Mary Lou Driedger

LOST

on the Prairie

LOST

on the Prairie

MaryLou Driedger

WANDERING FOX *An imprint of*
HERITAGE HOUSE PUBLISHING

Wandering Fox Books, an imprint of Heritage House Publishing Company Ltd.
heritagehouse.ca

Cataloguing information available from Library and Archives Canada

ISBN 978-1-77203-368-7 (pbk)
ISBN 978-1-77203-369-4 (ebook)

Cover and interior book design by Jacqui Thomas

The interior of this book was produced on 100% post-consumer paper,
processed chlorine free and printed with vegetable-based inks.

Heritage House gratefully acknowledges that the land on which we
live and work is within the traditional territories of the Lkwungen
(Esquimalt and Songhees), Malahat, Pacheedaht, Scia'new, T'Sou-ke, and
W̱SÁNEĆ (Pauquachin, Tsartlip, Tsawout, Tseycum) Peoples.

We acknowledge the financial support of the Government of Canada through
the Canada Book Fund (CBF) and the Canada Council for the Arts, and the
Province of British Columbia through the British Columbia Arts Council
and the Book Publishing Tax Credit.

25 24 23 22 21 1 2 3 4 5

Printed in Canada

Dedicated to my mother,
Dorothy Marie Schmidt Peters,
who had endless faith in me and
never failed to celebrate and
affirm me as a writer

Chapter 1

"HE'S NOT DOING IT. I won't allow it."

I'm yanked from my dreams by Mama's voice, louder than when she hits the highest hallelujah singing duets in church with Papa. Bits of moonlight dance on my quilt. It must be after midnight.

"Land sakes! Peter is only twelve years old. All kinds of dreadful things could happen to him."

I don't know how my little brother Alvin can still be snoring beside me. Mama's worry snakes up two flights of stairs and ricochets off the sloping ceiling of our attic bedroom.

"What if the train is robbed? What if the horses get sick? What if there's an early snowstorm?"

Mama's words conjure a thrilling scene: Two masked outlaws have their rifles pointed at my chest. The snorting of my horse Prince makes them turn their heads and I escape, only to get caught in a sudden blizzard. I am plowing through deep snow when Mama's sharp voice interrupts my imagination.

"Nein, nein, nein!" Mama insists. "He's not going."

Sometimes when she's hot and bothered Mama speaks German, the language of her childhood.

This is my last night in the farmhouse in Newton, Kansas, where I've lived since the day I was born. My family is moving to Canada. Tomorrow I, along with my brothers Levi and Sylvester, will begin a ride across the prairie on a slow freight train with our chickens, pigs, cows, horses, farm tools, pots and pans, and furniture. Papa only told me I'd be going along with my brothers this morning when we were milking the cows in the barn. I guess he told me before he told Mama.

"I just lost one son. I'm not going to lose another." Mama's voice is a touch quieter now but just as firm. "Peter can't go."

"Peter is strong and smart," says Papa, which makes me wiggle my toes under my quilt. "Besides, we haven't got a choice."

I sigh and bury my face in my pillow. We don't have a choice because my oldest brother, Herman, is over in the church cemetery. He was to ride in one of the train cars with the horses. Now I have to take his place.

Herman was eighteen years old and so excited about our family's move to Canada, but one February morning, when Mama went to wake Herman, he was dead in his bed. We don't know why. Papa called the postmaster, who does a bit of doctoring, but he just shook his head and said, "Might have been his heart."

We buried Herman during such a cold spell that we needed two wagonloads of hot coals to thaw the ground enough to dig his grave.

Herman had been reading a book called *Captains Courageous* out loud to Alvin and me. It was by a fellow named Rudyard Kipling. Every night, just before bed, we'd light the kerosene lamp and sit around the dining room table together. Herman's voice made the young boy Harvey's adventures at sea seem real as could be. The day Herman died we were about to finish the book.

After Herman's funeral Alvin and I took *Captains Courageous* up to our room. We sat on our bed, and I tried to read the last chapter aloud but the words on the page kept swimming away. When Alvin's tears started dripping onto my sleeve, I closed the book. Then he and I went down to the kitchen and ate till our stomachs near exploded. Folks had started bringing over food as soon as they heard about Herman dying.

Mama stayed in her room for six days after the funeral. Papa brought her things she loves—bowls of spicy beet borscht and slices of sweet peach pie; but Mama wouldn't touch a bite.

Alvin finally got her out of the bedroom. Alvin gets these shaking fits real regular, and Mama is the only one who knows what to do when his whole body starts trembling and the foam bubbles out the sides of his mouth. She jams a stick between his teeth and holds him just right so he doesn't bite his tongue or hurt himself too bad.

When Mama heard Alvin start thrashing and screaming, she bolted out of her room to his side and never went back.

But she doesn't smile anymore at breakfast and say, "What new adventures did you dream about last night, Peter?"

She doesn't call Alvin "my little man" when he runs errands for her. She doesn't even hum hymns while she's making supper.

WE DRIVE INTO NEWTON BEFORE dawn. A rucksack with some of my clothes and *Captains Courageous* is nestled in the straw in the back of the wagon. Sylvester and Levi rode our horses Prince and Gypsy down to the station near sunset yesterday, just after all the neighbours had circled onto our farmyard with their wagons to haul our belongings and animals into town. My big brothers stayed at the station for the night to watch over everything.

Mama is fearful quiet as we roll down the road lined with trees turning a dozen kinds of red and gold. Papa fills in the empty spaces with cheerful talk. "You're growing up, Peter. You can do this. I'd go myself, but I have to stay here and settle our loan at the bank and be sure everything is shipshape for the folks who've bought the farm. Mama and Alvin and I will board the passenger train and follow you in three days."

I nod every now and then as Papa talks, but it is hard to listen to his words because my heart is pounding so big and mighty I think my family might hear it. I am setting off on an adventure, and I can't wait for it to start.

Papa keeps giving instructions. "The train will stop in different cities and you will get out, buy something to eat, talk to your brothers, and see to the horses."

Alvin pipes up, "I'm glad you'll be with Prince and Gypsy, Peter, so they won't be lonely."

I smile at Alvin, who knows the horses are my good pals. It's been my job to feed and water them since I was his age.

When we arrive at the station, the train is already there, and Sylvester and Levi along with three of my uncles have loaded everything up. Alvin plugs his ears because our animals are setting off a fearsome racket, chickens squawking, pigs squealing, and cows bellowing. They are just as excited about the trip as I am.

The conductor, whose thick brown moustache almost hides his wide mouth, yells, "All aboard!"

Mama and Papa and Alvin go to Sylvester and Levi's cars near the engine to say goodbye, and then they walk down the platform to mine at the end of the train. Mama hands me an old sugar sack that smells of spicy pickles, smoked sausage, buttered bread, and her dried cinnamon apples. Then she hugs me, and her arms squish the air out of my lungs clear to my ribs. Two hot tears slip across her cheeks and slide down my neck.

I can tell Mama wants to say something. She gnaws her lips and opens them so wide I can see all of her teeth right to he back of her mouth, but only short gasps come up from her throat. Papa shakes my hand strong and steady, and then he puts his arm around Mama's shoulders and leads her away. She doesn't look back at me, but Alvin does.

"Bye, Peter!" he shouts and gives me a huge grin and a wave.

I wave back. "See you soon."

I plant both my hands on the edge of the railway car and swing my legs up into the pile of fresh straw. Prince and Gypsy nicker hello. Their eyes are wide as mine.

I can tell they're nervous about their strange surroundings because they've each already left a dump of dung under their tails. I grab the shovel propped in the corner of the railway car and quickly scoop up their mess and sling it outside.

"Careful, boy," hollers the conductor as he does a little dance around a steaming pile of horse droppings that land close to his feet.

"Ready for me to shut the door?" he asks. I nod and stand between Gypsy and Prince, holding both their manes tight as ever I can. The huge wooden panel slides shut and the conductor throws the bolt in place.

Light washes down through an opening in the ceiling. A whistle shrieks, metal screeches, and the train jerks forward so powerful I almost tumble.

Then we pick up speed, till we are hurtling like a pitcher's baseball down the tracks. Little streams of autumn wind rush in through the cracks in the car. Prince and Gypsy paw the straw with their hooves and toss their heads in excitement.

"Time for adventure!" I shout.

Chapter 2

IT'S A MITE CHILLY IN the railway car, and my stiff fingers are finding it hard to kink around Grandpa Hugo's puzzle. Grandpa connects nails in twisted ways to make puzzles exasperating to untangle. "In and out, over and under ... Dang it all."

"This one's called the Rattlesnake," Grandpa Hugo chuckled, slipping the puzzle into my pocket when I went to say goodbye to him. "Hope it doesn't drive you crazy on that long trip."

Grandpa's eyes shone bright. "Wish I was going with you, Peter. Don't let those cold Canadian winds blow your memories of Kansas clear out of your head. Remember there's still a warm southern family holding you close in prayers to the Almighty."

Grandpa Hugo shook my hand real firm and then emptied his nose into his handkerchief with a thundering snort. "*Gruss Gott*," he said. Go with God.

I get up to check on Gypsy and Prince. They are whinnying and pawing the straw.

"Something got you spooked?" I ask, rubbing their shaking shanks before sitting down again in the warmest corner of the railcar with Grandpa's puzzle. As I slip two nails apart I remember how Grandpa Hugo and I went gopher shooting one last time.

"Don't you worry none," said Grandpa, scanning the bare fall field. "There will be plenty of gophers up there in Canada."

"Do you think I'll get a penny at the general store for the tails like I do here in Kansas?"

"Might be, though I'll never understand why. Imagine the government paying people to shoot those chubby-cheeked grain robbers when any self-respecting farmer would finish them off for free." Grandpa Hugo shook his head.

"I'm glad there's a reward for killing gophers," I said. "When Herman and I went gopher shooting he'd give all the tails to me so I could trade them in for peppermint sticks or chewing gum at the store."

"You had a mighty fine brother, Peter." Grandpa put a hand on my shoulder. "Mighty fine."

Something is rattling Prince. He's knocked over his water bucket. I go to set it to rights, scratch his back the way he likes, and then sit down again. I take *Captains Courageous* out of my rucksack and stroke the cover, thinking about Herman.

Herman was my best pal. He taught me how to ride a horse and crack a chestnut open. It was Herman got me playing chess and showed me how to keep score in a baseball game. Thanks to Herman

I can catch a fish and recognize the call of the whistling duck. And thanks to Herman who up and died, I'm now travelling in this train car instead of him. I wipe away my tears with my shirtsleeve.

My mind and heart are so full of missing Herman, I don't notice right off that Prince and Gypsy have gone from being jittery to downright terrified! Driblets of pee leak down their legs. Their breath escapes in raggedy gasps, and the hairs on their backsides spike straight up. I click open Herman's silver pocket watch that Mama gave me after Herman died.

The hands say eight o'clock. I know we're due to stop in Omaha soon for a good long spell. Maybe Sylvester and Levi can help me figure out what's spooking the horses.

Gypsy kicks back just then, and the iron shoe on her foot bangs my knee.

"Owww!" I howl and clutch my knee to my chest. Blood spurts down my leg and soaks into my socks. Gypsy and Prince snort and toss hay back with their hooves. They are dancing from side to side so fast they rock the train car like it's the cradle Alvin slept in when he was a baby.

"What's going on?" I holler.

Prince turns his head to the right and I see his dark, wet eyes fixed on something curled along the far side of the railcar.

"A copperhead," I whisper. "What's a snake doing in here?"

Papa and I once discovered a nest of copperheads in a clump of trees alongside our pasture. Papa chopped their heads off clean and quick with a spade.

"They've got poison in those fangs Peter," warned Papa, as we stared at their dead limp bodies banded in different shades of brown. "It's a poison powerful enough to kill little Alvin or even Grandpa Hugo now that he's getting on in years. Better to get rid of these copperheads and be safe rather than sorry."

I know for certain the snake sliding towards me now is another copperhead but the shovel Papa left in the railcar is too far away for me to reach.

Will I get the snake all riled up if I move?

What should I do?

My mouth tastes dusty. Perspiration trickles from my hairline down over my forehead till it stings my eyeballs.

Just then, the copperhead strikes. Its body jerks forward and it snatches something out of the straw. A skinny tail sticks out one side of the copperhead's mouth. The snake isn't crunching down; it's just holding the creature whole, its fangs piercing the tiny body clean through.

This is my chance. I jump up and sprint across the swaying car to the shovel. I come up behind the snake. I raise the shovel high as my arms can stretch and slam its edge down swift and strong on the copperhead's neck. Wet slimy stuff oozes out into the straw.

I lay my head against Prince's broad, warm side and breathe in and out deep as I can. Then I edge closer to the snake. It isn't moving. Its orange eyes are blank.

A faint squealing has me hunkering down. There in the straw are seven tiny, wrinkled, pink-skinned creatures huddled close to their mama. Her eyes are wild and her whiskers are vibrating like the tightest string on Grandpa Hugo's guitar.

IT ISN'T LONG BEFORE THE train jolts to a halt and the conductor opens the door on the railcar. "Welcome to Omaha."

I'm sitting cross-legged on the floor. The dead snake is draped around my neck, and my blood-soaked pant leg is rolled up. Sylvester and Levi stand beside the conductor. Their mouths drop when they see me.

"What happened to you, Peter?"

"Are you hurt?"

"Where did that snake come from?"

"Why aren't you wearing your hat?"

Sylvester and Levi's questions rush off their tongues and fill the air with curiosity and worry.

I finger the snake's dead body slung around my neck. I unbend one leg so they can see the jagged cut with its scab just beginning to crust and pick up the hat I'm balancing in my lap. Moving nice and slow and gentle-like, I hold it out for them to see. It is filled to the brim with straw and seven blind, mewling gophers drinking milk from their trembling mama.

"Looks like you ain't been twiddling your thumbs on this trip so far, young man," says the conductor.

I tilt my head back and smile so big, my face near cracks wide open.

Chapter 3

A LADY WITH LIPS PAINTED raspberry red and hair all high and frizzy smiles and says, "Hello there, handsome fellow," as she waves her eyelashes up and down in my direction. Her dress collar is so low, I can see a whole lot of her bosom.

I can almost hear Mama's voice saying, "It's not polite to stare, Peter." But I think if she were here, Mama might be staring too.

Two men on the street clutch pistols slung around their waists. They shout things at each other that Mama would wash my mouth out with soap for saying.

In his Sunday sermons, Pastor Bartel's been known to thunder as he slaps the pulpit with his open palm, "Beware of the evil one waiting to pull you into dens of sin."

I kind of wonder if maybe I'm in a den of sin right now, because everywhere I look there's something that makes my heart gallop and my mind burst with questions.

The conductor announced the train would be in the Omaha station for six hours, so Sylvester and Levi decided we'd do some exploring. First, though, we took Prince and Gypsy out for a walk around the rail yard. Then we left them in the freight car with plenty of water, full pans of oats, and fresh straw to bed down in.

Levi tried to convince me to drown my gopher family in the barrel of water outside the train station.

"Those critters aren't going to survive the long trip to Canada anyway, Peter. It would be better to do away with them now."

I'm still thinking on that, but something won't let me kill that mama gopher and her babies, not after she's already seen one child die in a copperhead's mouth. It's befuddling, especially when I think about all of those gophers' tails Herman and I have traded in at the store, but for now I've made my little gopher gang a nest inside my food sack. It's got enough crumbs for the Mama gopher to nibble on for quite some time.

My brothers and I are making our way down Omaha's 16th Street, trying to dodge all the people out and about enjoying the day. A man wearing a dark suit and a straw hat calls out to us.

"Omaha Packers are playing today! Come inside and place a wager on the ball game!" Bouncy piano music is coming from the open door behind him and I'd like to go hear it, but Sylvester yanks me back as I take my first step towards the door.

"That's a saloon, Peter!" Sylvester shouts. "Mama would have a fit if you went in there. It's sure to have ladies of the evening and men all liquored up playing poker and gunslingers smoking cigars and maybe even a fortune teller."

"Is it a den of sin?" I ask Sylvester.

"I'm pretty sure it is," says Levi.

We turn off 16th Street down Pratt Street, and my brothers commence walking so fast I can't keep up.

I shout. "Hey! Wait! Sylvester, what's the hurry?"

"Conductor told us about the Krug Amusement Park on 52nd street. Now that'll be something, Peter. But we need to get there pretty quick if we want to have some fun before we head back to the train."

I'm panting by the time we spot a towering wooden frame outlined against the blue sky. It twists and turns like a giant-sized version of Grandpa Hugo's puzzles. Open cars race on tracks that plunge and swoop and surge straight up steep mountains.

"What is that?"

"It's a roller coaster, Peter," says Levi. "They call it the Big Dipper. Want to go for a ride?"

We stride into the park, which is as noisy and jam-packed as a cattle yard on auction day. Men crowd around tables toasting each other with foaming glasses of Krug's beer.

I see a sign with the words *Tunnel of Love* over a kind of cave on a waterway. Couples are climbing into little boats and rowing into the cave. "What will they do in there in the dark?" I ask Sylvester.

"You will find out when you're a little older, Peter ... but look up."

There in the sky is a giant red and yellow balloon with a basket under it. People are leaning over the edges waving to those of us down below.

I look up so long I get a crick in my neck. What would it be like to float that close to the clouds? My stomach dips and sways and my heart foxtrots with excitement just thinking about it.

"We don't have enough money for a ride in the balloon, Peter," says Sylvester, "but I sold my accordion to cousin Valentine before we left Newton, and you can have two bits if you want to ride the roller coaster."

"Don't you and Levi want to go?" I ask him.

Sylvester scratches behind his ear. "I don't think it's really for me," he admits, "and Levi says he's rather ride the Ferris wheel. I'll just watch you on the roller coaster, Peter."

I have to stand in line to get on the roller coaster, but I hardly notice time pass because there are dancing women on the stage nearby lifting their long legs high in the air and holding up their skirts while a band blares music. Suddenly a foot hits my behind so hard I kind of stumble forward. "Hey," I yell angrily and turn around to see a girl about my age, her face radish red.

"I'm ever so sorry!" Her freckled cheeks crumple up and her blue eyes wince. "I was trying to see if I could lift my leg as high as those ladies."

"Guess you can," I say, laughing, and then, remembering my manners, I stick out my hand.

"Peter Schmidt. I'm from Kansas."

"Nice to meet you, Peter. I'm Annie." She shakes my hand hard like she means it. "My Papa runs this roller coaster and he's letting me have a free ride tonight."

"My brother paid for my fare." I point at Sylvester and he gives me a wave and a grin.

When it's our turn to get on the roller coaster, a broad-shouldered, black-bearded worker who is opening the door of every car asks, "Mind if my girl Annie sits with you, son?"

"No, sir," I say, and Annie slides in next to me. Her brown hair smells like the lilacs growing round our house in Newton, and her petticoat tickles my leg. It makes me feel sort of squirmy but real good at the same time.

The car lurches forward, and Annie's fingers clutch my leg. I put my palm down on top of her hand and spikes of excitement speed to different parts of my body. I hardly notice we've reached the top of the first steep hill on the roller coaster frame.

As the car plummets like a falling star, Annie starts shrieking the way Mama did the time a family of bats swooped out of the root cellar.

"That first drop always terrifies me," Annie confesses once we reach the bottom of it. "Weren't you scared?"

I nod. Newton seems very far away as I tilt my chin up at the dusky sky. Is this really me? Peter Schmidt, riding a roller coaster in a strange city with a pretty girl beside me?

Just then, there's a skin-crawling screech and our roller coaster car stops so quick our chests lurch forward over the bar in front of us.

"What's wrong?" Annie looks down. "Oh no!"

The front car on one of the trains below us has crashed through the guard rail and teeters on the brink of the roller coaster frame. For a long moment, it hangs there balancing like one of those tightrope walkers I saw at the county fair. The screams coming from the people in the train below are sharp with terror.

And then the first car plunges off the edge, pulling along the three cars behind it. The lead car lands upside down on the ground with a thud that sends a rippling tremor through the whole frame of the roller coaster.

The other cars don't make it all the way to the ground and crash onto one of the lower tracks. Miraculously none of them flip over. They land like coins that have been tossed into a basket and all turn up heads.

"Look," Annie shouts pointing below us. "Papa is climbing the roller coaster frame. He is going to try and rescue those people."

Annie buries her face in my shoulder and grabs my neck as hard as Mama did at the station saying goodbye. "I can't watch," she says.

Annie's papa makes his way up to the derailed cars and, one by one, helps the people get out. He guides them as they climb down the roller coaster frame to the ground.

I can't tear my eyes away from the rescue being carried out down below, even though watching it is terrifying. I can see that some of the people have blood running down their faces. Annie's papa has two of the children crawl onto his back and he carries them to the ground. He does the same thing for a woman who seems to have broken her leg.

Once all the people from the crashed cars are safe, Annie's papa starts making his way up to our train. Annie is shaking and sobbing as she watches him. Her hand holding mine trembles.

We are in the last car of our train, so Annie's papa reaches us first. He squeezes her shoulder and gives me a confident nod before we begin the treacherous trip. Her papa's smooth, strong voice tells us where to carefully put our feet next and where to grasp the wooden frame with our hands.

In between these instructions he chants over and over in a low, rolling river of comfort, "Everything will turn out just fine."

Levi and Sylvester are waiting at the bottom of the roller coaster when my feet finally touch grassy ground. They each grab one of my hands.

"We've got to go, Peter!" shouts Sylvester. "We're going to miss the train." They start running, pulling me along with them. I twist my head around for just a second and see Annie being hustled away by an older woman. "Annie," I call out. She turns and gives me a little wave.

"Run, Peter. Run!" my brothers holler. I start to run, faster than I ever thought I could.

If we miss the train, what will happen to the chickens and pigs?

To Prince and Gypsy?

Will my gopher family survive?

And what will Mama say if the train shows up in Canada without us?

When we arrive at the train station, my lungs feel as huge and hot as the air balloons at the amusement park. I'm drenched with sweat.

The conductor shakes his head. "I was mighty worried about you fellows. We're pulling out directly."

Sylvester and Levi swing up into their cars and as I run down to mine, the last one on the train, I can hear them holler, "See you in Fargo."

I jump aboard and collapse in the straw. Before the conductor even slides the door shut, I'm asleep. I don't even notice when the wheels screech and we begin rolling north, but even in my dreams I can feel the train chugging along beneath my body like a lullaby following the beat of my snoring.

Chapter 4

"SAVE HER!" I SCREAM, AS Annie's wrist jerks from my handhold. She tumbles down from the roller coaster car. Her papa waits below, arms wide, boots rooted, but before I find out whether he catches her or not, I wake up.

I'm shaking. Curly threads of steam spiral from Prince and Gypsy's nostrils. Arrows of sun seep through the slits in the corners of the railcar, but they can't pierce the block of icy air trapping me.

I rub my head to erase the image of Annie falling from my mind. I shudder as I remember the people who dropped from the roller coaster last night with no chance of being caught in someone's open arms. I think about Annie. Will I ever see her again?

My crazy dream keeps bouncing around in my brain, so it is a few minutes before I realize the train isn't moving. Have we arrived in Fargo?

I expect the conductor will come and open the door soon. I'm awful hungry. The mama gopher has finished the last crumbs from my food sack, and we left Omaha in such a hurry that Sylvester and Levi didn't buy sandwiches and apples from the lady selling them outside the saloon like we planned.

It's powerful quiet. The train station in Omaha was louder than our churchyard after a wedding. Whistles shrieking, conductors hollering "all aboard," babies bawling, peddlers trying to out-bellow each other. But here there aren't any sounds at all. Is everyone in Fargo still sleeping?

I try doing Grandpa Hugo's puzzle, but my fingers are so cold they can barely move. I lace them together and bring them up to my lips to warm them with my breath. Why isn't the conductor coming?

"Hey! Open the door!" I get up and start pounding on the door with my fist. "Is anybody out there? I'm starving and freezing in here."

Has the conductor forgotten about me? If he has, surely Sylvester and Levi will come to let me out. Unless ... the conductor has forgotten about them too.

I flex my muscles and attack the huge wooden door panel, but it won't budge. I can see it is anchored shut on the inside because of a curved metal hook that has slipped into place through an iron loop. It looks an awful lot like a link in one of Grandpa Hugo's puzzles. I study it for a bit. If I could just get that metal hook up through the loop, maybe I could slide the door open.

I try hammering the hook with my fist till my skin tears and bruises stain my hand. I go check on my gopher family to see if they are staying warm.

But they look real cozy inside the sugar sack, snuggled deep in the crater I've made for them in the hay. Next to their nest I see the shovel I used to kill the copperhead.

I take it back to the door and start pounding on the metal hook with the shovel blade. It edges upward just a tiny bit with each ringing blow. I start counting one, two . . . and when I get to fifty the metal hook pops out of the loop. I fall backwards into the hay, exhausted. Prince snorts and Gypsy nudges me up with her nose.

I pull on the door and it opens just a sliver. I wedge my body sideways in the crack I've made and shove back. The door moves a little more. I give one last heave and the opening becomes wide enough for me to jump down out of the car.

My feet slip right out from under me as I land and I tumble down a rocky ravine. The jagged edges of stones rip my jacket and pants and scrape my skin as I bounce down, down, down like a ricocheting rifle bullet. I put out my foot to brace myself as I crash into a pine and lie there in a bleeding ball.

After a moment, I try to stand up, sliding my back along the wide tree trunk for support, but I sway and shake and when I open my eyes everything around me is spinning in blurry circles. My foot hurts something terrible. I stand like a crippled crane. Sweating and exhausted after just a few seconds, I sink back down on the rusty pine needles carpeting the base of the tree and shake my head to clear it.

Minutes later, I try to carefully rise again. My shoe is suffocating my swelling ankle. I look up, way up, at the train tracks at the top of the ravine I've landed in.

"Land sakes!" I scream.

The whole rest of the train is gone.

Not there.

Vanished.

The engine is gone.

The cars carrying my brothers are gone.

All the boxcars are gone.

My car sits alone on the tracks. I must be dreaming again, or maybe my fall has done something to my eyesight. I squeeze my eyes closed and count to ten and then look up again. No. The train has definitely disappeared.

I drop back down. I drag my legs up to my behind. My jacket and pants are so ripped from my rocky tumble down the ravine that I may as well be naked. My skin is shredded and in places thin strips of it twist like stringy noodles dangling from my bruised bones. There is scarcely an inch of my body that isn't pierced with pain.

Slowly, I raise my head again to my lonely railcar, and then I throw my head back and scream at the sky. "Herman, this is all your fault! Why did you up and die? If you hadn't, I wouldn't be here!"

I drop my head onto my bloodied knees. I start to cry in great gulping sobs that shake my shoulders and rattle my rib cage.

I CRY SUCH A LONG spell that eventually my tears dry up and even the slime from my nose stops dripping.

The sun is straight and true above me when my ears catch a faint neighing and nickering coming from the train car. It's Gypsy and Prince. They must be scared and worried and wondering where in the world I've got to.

My horses need me.

My gophers need me.

My mama needs me safe so she won't stay all sad forever.

My papa needs me to work with him, and he needs the horses even more, to help us start farming in Canada.

Surely Sylvester and Levi will send someone back to get me once they notice I'm gone, but will they find me way down here? I need to get back up to the train car somehow, and I have to do it before nightfall.

I scan the ravine. About thirty yards away, a steep path snakes up the slope. It's clear of trees and bushes and dirt packed. I drag myself over to a dead branch and pick it up to keep steady as I try to stand. The rough bark stings my palms, criss-crossed with cuts, but the branch gives me balance and keeps some of my weight off my ballooning ankle.

I shuffle over to the path and start climbing. I carefully count ten steps and then stop to rest. On parts of the trail where it is very steep, I sit down and wiggle myself up backwards so I won't lose my balance.

When I plop down about halfway up the slope I notice the bushes all around me are covered with gooseberries. I grab as many as I can and stuff them in my mouth. Their bitterness bites my tongue and their juice puckers the inside of my cheeks before it dribbles down my chin. I drop some of the berries in my pockets for the gophers and Prince and Gypsy.

As I walk, I keep my head down because looking at the steep climb ahead makes me dizzy. With my eyes to the ground I spy some hickory nuts and black walnuts. Maybe I can crack them open later in the railcar with my shovel. I carefully slide my shoe off my swollen foot and fill it with the nuts. Then I tie the shoe around my neck by the lace. My ankle feels better freed from its leather prison.

The sun is sinking huge and orange when I finally reach the tracks. I won't be able to get in on the side of the railcar where I left because there's a good chance I'd just tumble back down the ravine. I limp over to other side and open the door there using the iron handle.

Prince and Gypsy toss their manes, wave their tails and nicker loud and long to greet me. I feed them berries but I'm too tired to crack the nuts. I drop a few berries into the gopher sack, and then I lay my hands on Prince and Gypsy's broad backs.

"Let's lie down," I say. They obediently lower themselves to the floor of the railcar. The straw is mighty stinky from their dung and pee, but it doesn't matter. I cocoon myself between their warm, hairy bodies and quickly fall asleep.

Chapter 5

THE MINUTE I WAKE UP in the morning I know I have to get Gypsy and Prince out of this foul smelling boxcar and into the sunshine. In Omaha the conductor and my brothers easily placed a wide board to make a bridge to the ground from the railcar for the horses to walk down. Moving that heavy board in place all by myself is powerful tiring work. It takes me a long while and leaves me weak as a newborn calf.

My throat is dusty dry. My stomach is rumbling and rattling like a rusty truck engine. The crusted-over cuts on my body have stopped bleeding but some are oozing yellow and green stuff as thick as pond sludge. My ankle's still swollen and twisted.

I've got no real choice but to go looking for food and water. I'm not sure how far away we are from Fargo, but the soonest anyone will notice me missing is probably when the train gets there, and then who knows how long it will take to send someone back for me. I can't just wait around. I have to be strong and smart like Papa told Mama I was, and brave like Harvey grew to be in *Captains Courageous*. I have to find help.

Gypsy is my favourite horse. She seems to always know how I'm feeling and she'll give me a little nuzzle with her nose on my neck when I'm sad, or a nudge in my behind when I'm scared. But Prince is stronger, faster, and braver too when it comes right down to it. He can best carry me on his back and help me face whatever dangers lie out there over the rolling ridge in the distance. It is Prince I need to take to go for help and I need to leave Gypsy behind, hard as that may be.

After I get the horses outside, they start grazing on the grass growing fresh and full beside the tracks. I use the shovel to crack the nuts I found as I climbed up the ravine yesterday and I give them to my gophers. I know I have to let the gophers go. I have nothing more to feed their mama and no notion how long I'll be gone. They are so tiny they could easily be dead by the time I get back. I have to set them loose and hope their mama can find food and a safe place to dig a burrow where she can protect her babies.

So I take their sugar sack out of the railcar, lay it on the ground, and step away. The mama gopher comes out first, her head darting this way and that in the bright sun, and then her young ones scoot out and scatter like little bullets into the brush. Their mama races after them.

I don't even realize I am crying till the saltiness of my tears stings the scratches on my hand. "*Gruss Gott*," I whisper to my gophers, just the way Grandpa did when I left Kansas.

I'm wishing so bad I had a pencil and piece of paper, but I don't. I get my pocket knife and carve four words in the trunk of a white birch tree near the tracks. *Headed over ridge. Peter S.* The sun has moved straight up overhead by the time I'm done.

I loop one end of a rope around the tree with my message and then I tie the other end of the rope to the railcar door so people will be sure to see what I've written when they untie the rope.

I ponder long and hard about whether to tie Gypsy up or put her back in the railcar, but either way there's no chance of her setting off herself to find food or water if I don't come back, or of her escaping should some wild animal find her. I have to leave her free.

"Goodbye, Gypsy." I scratch her bony back with my fingernails the way she likes.

"Prince and I have to go and look for help or we might not be alive by the time we're found. But you've got to stay here, girl."

I grab Prince's mane with both hands and swing myself up on his broad back. He turns his neck around real slow to study me, but he stands solid as a soldier. He's not used to a rider. He's a wagon and plough horse, but he's so smart and steady that he'd never let a boy on his back vex him.

"Let's go, Prince." I gently push my heels into his sides.

After we walk a spell, I look back. Gypsy's head is up pointed in our direction. She's such a good girl. She hasn't even tried to follow us. I wonder what she must be thinking as she watches us move farther and farther away from her. I give her a wave, but I'm not sure she can see it.

It is a real nice fall day, not cold like yesterday morning. The friendly sun and my aching body get the better of me, so I lay my head down on Prince's scraggly mane as he plods on. I doze off a bit, rocked by the rhythm of Prince's steady steps.

My head jerks up when Prince comes to a sharp stop. We're on top of the ridge I saw in the distance from the train tracks. And below us on the other side is a lake as big and blue and beautiful as our flax field in full bloom.

"Land sakes! Look at all that water," I say to Prince. I run my dry tongue over my peeling, puckered lips and imagine how good a drink is going to taste.

Prince can't be hurried no matter how much I say, "Go on, boy." He just plods forward, down the gently sloping side of the rocky ridge towards the lake.

I FIGURE IT MUST BE late afternoon when we arrive at the shore. I slip off Prince's back and drop to the ground, stiff, sore, and plumb tuckered out. Prince clomps right up to lake and sinks his muzzle into its blue depths, sucking up the water and swallowing it in huge gusty gulps. After a bit, he rears his head up and swooshes water around in his mouth, streams of it pouring down from his tongue and teeth.

I'm not sure I have the strength to walk to the water, so I roll my body towards it lying lengthwise like a log and plop in with a big splash. The cold shoots through my limbs as I try to stand up. I'm thinking how fine the water feels on all my sores and cuts when I realize this lake doesn't slope gentle-like towards the middle. It's deep right at the edge. My toes can't touch bottom and I don't really know how to swim.

I splash my achy arms as my head sinks beneath the water. I manage to push myself up once, then twice, but the third time my head drops like a stone and I no longer have the strength to clear the surface. I begin to drift down towards the bottom of the lake. The water is clear and I can see fish and rocks and sea grasses. I'm floating like the hot-air balloon at the Omaha amusement park, except I'm in the water instead of the sky. I feel real peaceful-like and not even fretful about the fact that I am probably going to drown. I close my eyes and imagine I am Harvey in *Captains Courageous*, floating alone at sea after he has fallen off his father's ship.

Suddenly I feel something grab my arm. Then a pair of legs clamp tight around my waist the way that copperhead wrapped its mouth tight around the baby gopher. I am pulled up, up, up. I open my eyes and see a brown back, a long black braid, and a pair of arms slicing through the water like birds' wings pushing back the air to fly forward.

My rescuer's head breaks the surface of the water. He grabs my arm again and hauls me up till my head pops into the air. I gasp and gulp and sputter. I'm whacked on the back several times and water spurts from my mouth. Then those strong legs clinch my waist again and I am towed to the edge of the lake. My savior braces his arms and pulls his body out of the water. I do a complete flip in and out of the lake as he turns around without ever easing his scissor hold on my waist. He reaches down to encircle both my wrists with his bony fingers and flips me up onto the shore like a netted fish.

The man is breathing hard, his ribs moving in and out and his chest filling up and then collapsing like a pricked balloon. I don't know how he has enough spare breath to start shouting at me. My mind is all foggy and waterlogged, but I can hear the words "swim" and "foolish" and "enemy."

Enemy? Does this man think I am his enemy? Before I can even try getting up, he straddles my waist and starts pushing down on my chest with his big strong hands. Water dribbles out of my mouth as those hands press harder and harder, time after time. Is he trying to kill me?

Chapter 6

I'M FLAT ON MY BACK staring up at a giant. His spine is straight as the flagpole outside the Newton School. His eyes scan the ridgeline. His face looks kind of like my brother Herman's, with bony cheeks, a long nose, and a jaw that sticks out almost too far. He's wearing a loose leather shirt that has a flower design made from porcupine quills. Does he still think I'm his enemy? Could I get up quietly and slip away before he notices?

As if he's read my mind he turns and says, "You cannot swim, but you go in Enemy Swim Lake?"

I gulp. "Enemy Swim is the name of the lake?"

The man nods.

"That's a mighty strange name."

"Long ago a band of warriors from an enemy nation attacked while our people were asleep. The Dakota fought and forced the enemy to flee to the lake and swim away to an island. So the Dakota call it Enemy Swim Lake."

"Are you Dakota?" I ask, sitting up and looking my new acquaintance right in the eye.

"I speak Dakota. I am from the Sisseton-Wahpeton bands."

"But you're talking English."

"I learned at school."

"You went to school?"

"My grandfather wanted us to have book learning. He claimed property near the school."

"I went to school too," I say with a smile. "In Kansas."

"Kansas is far. Where are your parents?"

"Not certain exactly, but they are on a train going to Drake, Saskatchewan, in Canada. Our family is moving there."

"And you did not go with them?"

"I was on a different train with our horses."

The man points to where Prince is standing near his own horse, a black mustang several hands higher than Prince.

"Your horse is a fine one."

"His name is Prince. I left my other horse, Gypsy, behind at the railroad car. I'm awful worried about her being there alone."

"Why did you leave the train?"

"I didn't. It left me. I woke up yesterday morning and the whole train had disappeared except for my car. I was all alone on the tracks."

My new friend frowns. "Your car broke from the train?"

"I don't know. The next stop the train was going to make was in Fargo. I figure that's when my brothers will find out I'm gone and maybe send someone back to get me. They were in different train cars with the pigs and chickens and such. But it could take a fair bit of time."

"Then you will come home with me."

"To your house?"

"Yes. I have a son about the same age as you. His name is Joe. I am Arden Little Thunder."

"Peter Schmidt," I stick out my hand to shake his. "Thank you, Mr. Little Thunder, for saving my life. My mama and papa would thank you too if they were here."

Mr. Little Thunder nods. "You will ride home on my horse. When did you last eat?"

"I finished the food Mama sent along a good while ago. Yesterday, all I had were a few berries I found in the ravine near the train tracks."

Mr. Little Thunder walks over to his horse and opens a pouch dangling from the saddle. He reaches in and comes back to me carrying a small red square of something in his hand.

"Eat this."

"What is it?"

"Buffalo biscuit."

I've never heard of a buffalo biscuit, but I take a small bite just to be mannerly. "Hey. This is good. There are berries in it. It tastes like turnips."

Mr. Little Thunder nods and points to my hands. "Those cuts pain you?"

"They do hurt some, but not like my ankle. I twisted it when I rolled down the ravine yesterday."

"My mother has medicines. I will carry you."

Mr. Little Thunder turns and crouches down in front of me.

I wrap my legs around his waist and grasp his shoulders, broad and strong as Papa's. Mr. Little Thunder gets up real easy-like and strides over to his horse. That mustang stands still as stone while his master settles me in the saddle. Mr. Little Thunder swings himself up behind me and we trot off moving east along the trail by the lake. Prince follows us.

The sun is going down and Mr. Little Thunder urges the horse into a gallop. A chilling breeze sneaks under my torn shirt and sets me to trembling almost like my brother Alvin does when he's having one of his fits. Mr. Little Thunder must think I'm going to fall off the horse because he wraps one of his hard ropey arms around my chest and holds both the reins with the other. I'm shaking something frightful by the time the horse finally stops. Strong hands lift me down from the saddle. My mind is all fuzzy, and funny shapes are floating in front of my eyes.

I think I must be falling asleep, but things keep waking me up and I can never quite climb out of the strange world I seem to be slipping through. I can sense my body being lowered onto a bed, but when I open my eyes, I see Herman being lowered into his grave in the church cemetery in Newton. Water washes my cuts and sores, but when I open my eyes to see who is doing it, I see Mama at a strange-looking train station, tears spilling down her face. I can feel the weight of blankets pressing down on my chest, but when I try to shove them off, a vision of my mama gopher appears. She's biting the claw of an eagle with her babies trapped beneath it. I feel someone trying to push a spoon with hot liquid between my teeth, but in my mind I see a giant one of Grandpa Hugo's puzzles, a puzzle so tricky I will never twist my way through it.

I must fall asleep for real after that, because the next thing I know, I'm opening my eyes.

Sunlight washes in through a window. I'm lying in a bed.

I can see my toes sticking out of the grey blanket covering the rest of me. I look around. Eight faces stare at me. They belong to people of all shapes and sizes ringed around my bed. Is this another one of the strange things I was seeing last night?

No, these people are real. Just then, one of them, a young woman, laughs. A teenage boy coughs and a little girl starts to cry. Then I recognize Mr. Little

Thunder. He's right at the end of the bed. I raise my eyes to look at him. He lifts one bushy black eyebrow.

"You have decided to wake, Peter."

Chapter 7

I'VE BEEN STAYING WITH THE Little Thunder family for nigh unto a week now. Mr. Little Thunder went to fetch Gypsy from the train car my second day here.

He left before sunrise, and it was almost dark when he returned. Gypsy looked all tuckered out as she trooped into the yard. I wiped away fierce tears with the back of my hand at the sight of her. When she spied me she neighed and nickered and pawed the ground with her hooves.

"Ah, sweet Gypsy," I crooned as I combed my fingers through her mane the way she likes. She blew deep fluttery sighs out her nostrils. Even though my body still ached all over, my heart felt a whole lot better knowing Gypsy was safe and back with Prince and me.

Mr. Little Thunder got off his mustang. "Stood right by the train car," he said, nodding at Gypsy.

"That's where I told her to stay."

Mr. Little Thunder rubbed Gypsy up and down the side of her neck and whispered something to her in Dakota.

Then he looked at me as if he knew what I was about to ask next. "No one was there."

"No one had carved a reply message under mine on the tree or left footprints in the dirt?"

Mr. Little Thunder shook his head.

"I can't believe someone isn't looking for me by now."

"We will find your family." Mr. Little Thunder started walking his mustang to the corral, and I followed behind with Gypsy.

Joe, Mr. Little Thunder's youngest son, looks much like his father except his hair is a good deal shorter and he's more prone to smile and laugh than his papa. Joe's been mighty friendly to me. He goes to school during the day, and when he comes home, I help with his chores and then he takes me rabbit hunting or we play with his two big dogs, Wi and Hanwi. Joe told me their names mean sun and moon in Dakota.

The dogs love to wrestle and try to nip your nose. Sometimes we use an old horse harness to hook them up to a cart that Joe's grandfather made and they take us for rides. Many of Joe's relatives live in houses nearby, and in the evenings we play baseball with his endless supply of cousins. My brother Herman and I used to love to toss the ball around and practise our batting swing by hitting stones out into our cornfield in Kansas with long sticks. But it's more fun to play with so many kids. Last night, there was near to twenty of us.

Today's Saturday and Joe doesn't have school.

"Can Peter and I ride?" he asks his father after breakfast.

Mr. Little Thunder walks right over to the corral and brings out two horses, Prince and one of his mustangs.

The sun is bright, and as Joe and I canter across the prairie, I feel the air blow sharp and cool against my face. A honking flight of Canada geese wings its way over our heads as we pull up short at the bottom of a huge grassy hill.

"Race you to the top," Joe hollers sliding off his mustang's back.

Joe beats me easy. It takes me quite a spell to get up to the top. I've not healed completely from my tumble down the ravine and my near drowning, so I'm breathing awful heavy when we reach the highest spot. But it is worth the climb because it's so dang pretty in every direction you look. Fall forests on fire with oranges and reds, meadows high with golden grasses, silver twisting rivers, and deep blue lakes all spread out like the splashes of colour on my bed quilt back in Newton, the one my Mama made me.

I let out a whistle, long and low. "What a pretty place. It near takes my breath away."

Joe nods and then sits down and opens the sack he has tied to his belt. He hands me some fry bread and pemmican. I've been eating all kinds of new foods now that I'm staying with Joe and his family. Joe's grandmother is a fine cook. The fry bread we're devouring is different from my Mama's bread, but delicious. The pemmican is dried deer meat that Joe's grandmother pounds fine and mixes with bear fat and berries. I swipe my tongue all around my lips to make sure I get every little last bit of it in my mouth.

After lunch, we wind our way back down the hill, mount our horses, and gallop off to a hollow about a mile away. Joe stops at its edge and slides off his mustang.

"This hollow has many spirits," he tells me.

"How do you know there are spirits in there?" I ask.

"Everyone knows," says Joe. "We call this place Sica."

"Sica?" I ask.

"Means unhealthy in Dakota."

"You mean the spirits that live here aren't good spirits?" My voice squeaks with excitement. "Have you seen them?"

"No, but Grandmother tells stories about the spirits."

"What does she say?" I slip off Prince's back.

"She speaks of a monster named Hand who came to the people camped in Sica Hollow."

"What do you know about him?"

"He used dark ways to turn all the young men into killers. They murdered travellers passing by."

"That's awful."

"The medicine man asked the Creator for help. He sent a spirit named Thunder."

"Hey, that's part of your family's name."

Joe nods proudly. "The Thunder Spirit is mighty and strong."

"Does the Thunder Spirit have something to do with storms?"

"Yes. The Thunder Spirit brought powerful rains. During the storm, he trapped the monster Hand in vines, filled his mouth with water, and dug out his eyes."

"What a horrible way to die." A shudder rolls from my shoulders down to my toes.

"The rains flooded the hollow. Everyone in the camp drowned except one girl named Fawn."

"How did she survive?"

"She ran to the top of that hill we just climbed and was saved. But the spirits of all the dead still haunt the hollow."

"Let's walk through the hollow," I say excitedly.

"Why?" asks Joe.

"To show how brave we are. Come on, let's go."

Joe heads into the hollow without saying another word and I follow. We haven't walked far before Joe turns around and speaks so soft I can hardly hear him, "Be quiet. Your noise will disturb the spirits."

"But I wasn't saying anything," I whisper.

"The ground talks when you walk. You crack twigs with every step."

"Sorry."

I watch as Joe moves forward in a crouch, his eyes to the ground, sliding his feet over wet leaves cautiously, picking twigs up and moving them deliberately when he has to.

I hunker down like him and try to step real careful. It helps that I'm wearing a pair of moccasins Joe's mama gave me when she noticed how hard it was to fit my shoes over my swollen ankle. My ankle feels much better now, but I've kept the moccasins 'cause I've grown so used to wearing them. Their soft soles slip easily over the forest floor.

Joe's story has me spooked but good, and every time we pass a hollow log or a large rock I get a little thrill thinking a spirit will come sailing out.

Joe stops when we reach a gurgling spring. The water is a reddish colour.

"It might be poisonous," Joe says. "Don't touch it or drink it."

Joe looks up and inhales a deep fast breath that fairly trembles with wonder.

"Look, Peter," he whispers. "Up ahead. Have you ever seen such a thing?"

There in front of us, blanketing every tree branch in sight, hovering over rocks, perched on flowers and clinging to grass stalks are thousands and thousands of orange and black butterflies.

"What are they doing here?" I ask softly.

"Stopping for night. On their way to Mexico for winter."

"Land sakes! That's a longer trip than the one my family is making from Kansas to Canada."

"Let's get up a little closer."

Joe takes two steps forward and stops. He turns around, his eyes wide and wild.

"I can't move! My feet are stuck! I'm sinking. Help me, Peter!"

Chapter 8

"PETER, YOU SHOULD GO FOR help."

"I don't think so, Joe. By the time I come back you may have sunk in over your head."

"Won't happen."

"How do you know?"

"Father says as long as you don't fight it, quick-sand won't swallow you."

"But how will you get free?"

"Someone will have to pull me out."

"I can try. I'll get the horses and bring them here. They have ropes wrapped round their saddle horns."

I make my way back to the hollow entrance where we've left the horses. I don't worry now about walking quietly. If the spirits want to come and get me, they can. I'm more scared for my friend Joe than I am of spirits. I guide Prince through the trees till we get back to the quicksand. The mustang follows us.

I unwind the rope from Prince's saddle and make my way carefully over to Joe. "I'm back."

"Don't get too close," warns Joe.

I toss the rope out to Joe and he ties it tight around his body.

I plant my feet firm as tree roots and pull. I pull till the newly healed wounds on my palms break open and leak blood. I pull till my legs and arms feel like they are being ripped in two.

"I haven't moved," says Joe.

"How about I get Prince to help?"

As I twist the rope around Prince's saddle, I mutter in his ear, "You and me together, pal. We're a team. We can get Joe out."

"Pull, Prince," I order, and he starts moving forward. I grab the rope too and add the last bit of the strength I have left to the effort.

"Moved a little," says Joe.

"Pull harder, Prince," I shout. Prince's hooves are trying to move forward, but it is hard for him to get his footing with wet leaves and rocky earth all around.

"I have to go for help, Joe. But it will soon be dark and I don't want to leave you here alone."

"Leave Prince. You take the mustang. He knows the way home."

"Won't you be scared?"

"Got all the butterflies for company."

I look at the colourful creatures. Some are cradled in the blooms of flowers, their petals closing up around their wings for the night. Others have formed a huge black and orange flying carpet between tree branches. A few have even landed lightly on the quicksand around Joe.

"Butterflies bring good luck," Joe assures me. Only a slight quaver in his voice makes me realize he's probably a sight more scared than he's letting on.

"I'm going to leave the rope around Prince's saddle so you two will stay connected while I'm gone," I say.

"Watch over Joe," I tell Prince. He lifts his head and looks at me in a chiding way as if to say he knows his job and I needn't remind him. I mount the mustang and grab the reins.

"*Gruss Gott*," I say to Joe.

"What's that mean?"

"It's a German blessing my family uses."

"*Taŋyáŋ ománi*," says Joe. "It is the way we say 'good luck on your journey' in Dakota."

Joe keeps chanting the words as I ride off. "*Taŋyáŋ ománi, Taŋyáŋ ománi. Taŋyáŋ ománi.*" His voice gets quieter and quieter as the mustang picks his way through the trees and we finally leave the hollow.

It's definitely dusk, but I can still see the outline of the hill Joe and I climbed earlier. I figure we will head that way but the mustang has other ideas and he veers south and trots alongside a ridge. Joe said he knew the way home, so I loosen my hold on the reins and let him have his head. He is surefooted and breaks into a gallop. I hang on for the ride, as evening darkens the sky. The stars are bright and plentiful, the moon a huge orange circle. My grandfather told me looking at a full moon for too long a time can make you crazy. I decide I won't take any chances and keep my eyes looking straight ahead between the mustang's black-tipped ears.

Then I hear a sound that begins low and throaty and builds up to a full-blown howling. Despite Grandfather's warning I jerk my head up towards the sound to take a quick look. On the ridge to my right is near to a dozen coyotes, their noses pointing up at the moon and their mouths open wide. That canine choir is some comfort to me and takes me away from thinking about Joe and what could be happening to him.

We had coyotes at home in Kansas too, and on summer nights our whole family would gather on our front porch in the darkness and wait for the them. The first kid to hear one would give a loud shush and whisper, "Listen. Coyotes." And then we'd sit there with the warm night wrapped around us like a comfortable quilt listening to that fine prairie music. Sometimes when the coyotes were done, Mama would start in on a hymn in her soaring soprano, and Papa would join her with his down-deep bass, and then all us kids and Grandpa would chime in too. We had a pretty fine family choir. I wonder if I will ever sing in that choir again.

The mustang's not even spooked by the coyote's yowling. He just keeps galloping. It's as if he knows we need to hurry and get help for Joe.

And then I hear hooves pounding. Sounds like a stampede of horses coming towards me. I wonder if they are a wild bunch. The hooves suddenly silence and I hear Mr. Little Thunder's voice echoing through the darkness, "Joe, Peter, Joe, Peter, Joe, Peter," over and over and over again.

"I'm here!" I holler, loud as I can. "I'm here. I'm here." It isn't long before Mr. Little Thunder and a whole bunch of Little Thunder relatives ride into view.

"Peter? That you?" Mr. Little Thunder shouts.

"Yes. I was coming for help. Joe and I were in Sica Hollow and he got stuck in some quicksand."

Mr. Little Thunder turns to the other riders. "Let's go. Peter, climb up behind me. The mustang is tired. He'll find his way home."

I slide off the mustang and give his rear a friendly pat that sets him off. Mr. Little Thunder reaches down, and I grab his arm and swing up behind him on his stallion. It's getting cold and I'm glad for the warmth of Mr. Little Thunder's body on the saddle as we ride.

I'm thinking how cold Joe must be getting. I hope he's stayed still and not panicked. I hope those coyotes haven't scared him. I hope a bobcat or a bear hasn't found him, or one of the spirits of all those dead people that haunt Sica Hollow.

It isn't long before we reach the hollow's edge. "Leave the horses and walk," Mr. Little Thunder orders.

The riders all pull kerosene lanterns out of their saddlebags and strike matches to light them.

Mr. Little Thunder has one for me too.

"You lead the way, Peter," he says, and he and I step to the front of the line of bobbing lights snaking through the hollow.

It's so dark that it's hard for me to be sure exactly where Joe and I walked before, but when we come to the gurgling spring with the rusty water I know I've been leading the rescue party in the right direction.

I start calling out, "Joe. We're here."

Then the others start shouting Joe's name too.

Mr. Little Thunder holds up his hand to quiet us. He's heard something.

There's a low moaning somewhere ahead. It sounds the way my brother Alvin did once when he ate too many strawberries and had a stomach ache all night.

Then a groaning is added to the moaning as if the wind suddenly came up and set all the tree branches to creaking and cracking. Only thing is the air is still. There is no wind.

"What is it?" I whisper to Mr. Little Thunder. He puts a finger to his lip and shakes his head, and that's when the wailing starts. It's so sad it cracks your heart. It reminds me of the way Mama went on and on and on when Herman died.

I'm truly scared now. Poor Joe.

Has Hand come to claim him and turn him into a murderer like he did to those other boys?

Have the troubled spirits of the people who drowned returned? Have the coyotes streaked down to circle round him?

"THE SOUND IS FROM THERE," Mr. Little Thunder points to his right. Now he takes the lead and we all follow him.

My heart is squeezed tight and barely beating. Could that have been Joe moaning and groaning and wailing? Will he still be alive when we reach him?

And then Mr. Little Thunder is crashing through the trees and I can't keep up. When I reach him he is kneeling down beside Joe's body, mumbling all soft and tender as if he is praying: "*Cunwintku, cunwintku, cunwintku*, my son, my son, my son."

Joe is no longer in the quicksand. He is lying just as still as can be. Prince stands at Joe's head nuzzling his hair. Bunches of butterflies are perched on Joe's muddy pant legs, on his toes, on his bare arms, and along the rope still wrapped around his chest and still attached to Prince's saddle horn.

As Mr. Little Thunder bends his head to lay his ear on Joe's chest, the butterflies rise slow and gentle as morning fog and flutter off.

"He's alive!" Mr. Little Thunder shouts. He unties the rope around Joe's chest, then picks Joe up and drapes him over his shoulders. All of us turn, and we begin the trek out of the hollow. Moonlight streaks through the trees around us and casts eerie shadows on our bodies.

I'm walking just in front of Joe and his papa, and I can hear Joe muttering, "They came for me. They came for me."

Then he says it louder and louder.

"They came for me. They came for me."

Mr. Little Thunder stops and lays Joe down on the ground again. To our surprise, Joe lifts his hand to rub his head and then sits up. Mr. Little Thunder puts his arm around Joe's back.

"They came for me."

"Who came for you?" I ask.

"The spirits. They were swirling all around me in the quicksand, moaning and groaning and wailing. I couldn't see them but I could feel them and hear them. And then suddenly I was being pulled."

"By Prince? You still had the rope around you," I remind him. I don't even wait for Joe to answer I'm so worried. "Did the spirits try to hurt you?"

"I don't think they could because thousands of butterflies came gliding down and covered my body to protect me. I turned my head to look at Prince and a young girl was sitting in his saddle and riding him forward."

"But Prince wasn't strong enough to pull you out before."

"I know. But with that girl on his back he did."

"What did she look like?"

"She was Dakota, about my age, in a buckskin dress with a beaded belt around her waist. She smiled at me. Then Prince lurched forward and I was out of the quicksand. It took me a minute to catch my breath, and when I looked around again, Prince was still there but the girl was gone."

"Who do you think she was?"

"I don't know," Joe shakes his head.

"Could it have been Fawn?" I wonder aloud, "The only one of the Sica Hollow people to survive the fight between Hand and the Thunder Spirit?"

"Perhaps so," says Mr. Little Thunder. "You need to get home, Joe. Can you walk?"

"I'll try, Father," says Joe as we help him to his feet.

Joe walks a little slow but he does just fine. We've got a long trek back through the twisted trees and over the trails covered with wet leaves. Even once we reach the horses, it will be a fair ways home in the dark and cold. Lots of time for me to think about what's happened tonight and all the other adventures I've had since leaving the train station in Kansas.

Just a couple weeks ago I'd never been farther from our family farm than Newton, two miles away, and I'd never known anything but doing farm chores and going to school and church and visiting our neighbours who lived all round. Will Mama and Papa and Alvin even believe me when I tell them about the copperhead and the roller coaster accident, my near drowning in Enemy Swim Lake, and now my night in Sica Hollow?

Why, I'm almost like Harvey in *Captains Courageous*! I've not looked into the eye of whale or witnessed a fishing schooner being cut in half by an ocean liner. I haven't been lost in thick fog at sea or been haunted by a dead sailor like Harvey was, but I've sure been having some adventures! No doubt about that.

Chapter 9

THE NEXT MORNING, I POKE my head into Joe's room on my way downstairs. He is still fast asleep. I guess he is plumb tuckered out from yesterday's adventure. Mr. Little Thunder comes into the kitchen as I'm eating fry bread and honey.

"Come out to the barn," he says to me. I gulp down the rest of my food and follow him.

In the barn Mr. Little Thunder is giving the mustang I rode yesterday another rub down.

"I can't ever thank you enough, Mr. Little Thunder, for taking me and my horses in."

Mr. Thunder nods but he is frowning. What is on his mind?

Has his family had enough of me?

Are they going to ask me to leave?

Does Mr. Little Thunder blame me for what happened to Joe yesterday?

Mr. Little Thunder gets some water for the horses from the pump and fills the trough in front of them. He looks at me.

"Yesterday you acted as a brother would."

I start to shovel horse manure out of the stalls and put it in a wheelbarrow Mr. Little Thunder has placed nearby. He looks at me.

"I will get you back to your own brothers."

"Should we go to the railroad car once more and check if someone has been there?"

"I did."

"And had someone been there?"

Mr. Little Thunder shakes his head.

"I can't believe that," I say and I hurl a shovelful

of horse dung that misses the wheelbarrow and lands with a splat on the floor.

Mr. Little Thunder takes a rake and starts to spread out hay in each horse stall. I go over to clean up the mess I've made.

"Your family could be having troubles," he says.

"So what are we going to do?"

"There's people in Sisseton who have your name, Schmidt."

"Do you know them?"

Mr. Little Thunder shakes his head. He comes over to me and hands me a small square torn from an old newspaper. It's an advertisement.

I read aloud. "Wanted. Good girl that can sew to help in Schmidt's Dress Shop and Millinery. $3.00 a week."

"That's my name for sure," I say, "but Papa and Grandpa never talked about relatives in South Dakota. Where did you get this ad?"

"Went to Sisseton for flour and bullets a couple months back. Picked up a newspaper."

"And you just happened on this ad?"

"The name jumped out at me yesterday morning when I took a piece of old newspaper to start a fire in the stove."

"Have you ever seen this millinery shop?"

"The lady who runs it is married to Henry Schmidt, the miller. It should have come to mind when you spoke your name."

"So you think we'd best go and talk to them?"

Mr. Little Thunder nods. "We can head out tomorrow early. Sisseton is a fair way away."

"Is there a train station in Sisseton?"

"Yes."

"Should we stop there and check if they've received word about my missing train car?"

"Yes." Mr. Little Thunder picks up Prince's foot and turns up his hoof to clean it.

"Will I be coming back here?"

"Not sure. Depends what we learn."

"So tonight could be my last night here?"

"Might be."

"Then I may only have one more day with Joe?"

Mr. Little Thunder nods and picks up Prince's other hoof and starts to clean it. After he leaves the barn I stay for a spell. I lean on the railing between the horses' stalls.

I'm not sure how I feel. I know I need to do something to get back together with my family. The rest of my train, and my parents' train, are bound to have arrived in Saskatchewan already, and my Mama must be going crazy with not knowing where I am. But I've come to feel safe here with the Little Thunders, and Joe is starting to become almost as fine a friend as my brother Herman was to me.

I stand between Prince and Gypsy just breathing in their warm comfort for a minute or two.

"We've sure been having some adventures," I say to them. "Guess we might be in for more."

Prince and Gypsy move their heads up and down as if they are agreeing with me.

"WE'RE TAKING THE WAGON," MR. Little Thunder informs me when I step outside the next morning. "I need to bring back supplies."

Joe's mother has filled a sack with food for us and when I see it on the wagon seat I get a little catch in my throat because it reminds me of the dried apples and smoked sausage and buttered bread Mama gave me when I left Newton. That seems so long ago. It sure would be fine to taste some of my Mama's cooking again.

It's still dark when we roll off down the road. Gypsy and Prince follow along at our slow and steady pace. I said goodbye to everyone last night and hardly slept a minute, excited and wondering about what today might bring.

Mr. Little Thunder and I don't say much on the trip. There's a real chill in the air, and although the buckskin jacket and leggings Joe's grandmother made me keep my body warm, I rub my ears and nose every few minutes to keep their tips from freezing.

The steam from the horses' bodies rises up like a fog, covering Mr. Little Thunder and me.

I think about my last day with Joe. We had a fine time. We wrestled with Wi and Hanwi. We played catch. We lay on the grass for a long while and I told Joe the story of *Captains Courageous*. He said it was a wondrous tale. Joe's mother made a supper of venison stew. At nightfall we sat on a big rock near the house staring at the stars a spell before Joe and I shook hands real solemn and silent-like and headed off to bed.

Mr. Little Thunder and I pull up to the Sisseton train station about noon. I jump down from the wagon to follow Mr. Little Thunder inside. There's a passel of people lined up at the ticket window and they all turn to stare as we walk in. Mr. Little Thunder waits till everyone has attended to their business before he approaches the window motioning for me to follow.

"This is Peter Schmidt," he says, introducing me to the ticket agent, who scratches his grey moustache and pushes his wire glasses up to the top of his balding head.

"He was travelling to Canada. Found his train car five miles or so from Enemy Swim Lake."

"Have you heard about me?" I say, interrupting. Mr. Little Thunder speaks so slow and careful-like, and I'm in a hurry to know if this man has any news.

The ticket agent drums his fingers on the counter in front of him and ignores my question. He looks at Mr. Little Thunder. "What's the boy doing with you? He don't look like a Dakota to me."

"I found him near Enemy Swim Lake. Took him to my place."

"And when was this?"

"A week ago."

"Well, it just so happens I did get a message on the telegraph about that missing car. Head office in Minneapolis is sending an engine to retrieve it this coming Monday. They'll pull in here first thing in the morning and then head out to the line near the lake."

"That's great news!" I shout. "Did the message say anything about a missing boy?"

"No."

"Could you send word telling them a passenger from that lost train car will be waiting here at the station to be picked up?"

"Guess I could. What's your name again, boy?"

"Peter Schmidt," I say.

The ticket agent writes my name on a piece of paper with a pencil and says, "We've got some Schmidts here in town. Henry, the mister, runs the mill and his wife Euphemia has a nice little sewing business."

"We know," says Mr. Little Thunder.

"Could be this young lad could stay with them over the weekend. It'd save you making the trip back. Euphemia and Henry are good folks and though their house isn't big, they could probably spare a place for this fellow in their barn."

We find the sewing shop and millinery no problem. A tiny silver bell rings as Mr. Little Thunder opens the door and a woman sails out from behind the store counter to greet us. She's tall, with hair piled high on her head.

"How can I help you?" she asks. She's got a little pucker between her eyebrows that are lifted high. Guess she's wondering what two fellows are doing in a ladies' shop.

Mr. Little Thunder introduces both of us, and I explain what has happened to me.

"Mr. Little Thunder thought you might know something about my family since we share the same last name," I say as I finish my tale.

"Can't say for sure, but it seems to me my husband, Henry, did have some cousins down Kansas way," says Mrs. Schmidt as she smooths her long black skirt with her right hand and then straightens a frill on her white blouse with the left.

"Obliged if he could stay with you," Mr. Little Thunder says politely.

Mrs. Schmidt is frowning slightly and I try to reassure her. "It is just till Monday when the railroad fellows are coming from Minneapolis to pick up my train car."

Mr. Little Thunder adds, "He's got two horses. I can board them at the livery."

Mrs. Schmidt gives just a hint of a smile. "No need. I suspect we can do our Christian duty by this boy and his horses."

"Girls," Mrs. Schmidt calls in a voice that almost screeches. Three girls trot immediately into the shop from a door behind the counter, where they must have been listening to every word we said. The oldest looks to be about my age. The girls have matching blue checked dresses with wide white collars like a sailor would wear. Big white bows bounce in their hair. They line up in front of me from shortest to tallest.

Mrs. Schmidt introduces her daughters. "This is Ettie, Ellie, and Eudora."

"Pleased to meet you," Mr. Little Thunder and I say almost in unison.

"Girls, this is Peter Schmidt. He just may be a relative of your pa's. I want you take Peter and his horses up to the house. Show him the barn and have him put his things in the hayloft. He can sleep there tonight."

"Thank you," says Mr. Little Thunder.

We step out onto the street, and Ettie, Ellie, and Eudora follow. Mr. Little Thunder puts a hand on my shoulder.

"Goodbye and good fortune, Peter."

"Thanks, Mr. Little Thunder. I sure do appreciate all you've done for me."

Mr. Little Thunder jumps up into the wagon. I hold tight to Prince and Gypsy's reins as he pulls away. I feel like crying, but there's no way I'm going to do that with those three girls staring as if I'm the main act in a vaudeville show.

As he turns the corner by the train station Mr. Little Thunder stops and gives me a nod and a tiny bit of a smile. I wave back. Swallowing hard I turn to the three girls.

"I'm ready."

Chapter 10

LAND SAKES, CAN THOSE SCHMIDT girls ever talk! A waterfall of words gushes from their mouths as we walk into the red barn behind their house.

"My Grandpa built this barn, you know," Ettie says sweeping her arms upward to trace the arc of the high rafters. The sun is streaming in through the open door and little bits of hay dust and chicken feathers and horsehair float in its light. "Grandpa died three years ago from the consumption, buried over in the church graveyard there beside Grandma. They've got ever such nice gravestones. Papa paid for them himself since his brother Ben couldn't help out."

Eudora picks up the story as we climb up to the loft. She's pulled a thick grey blanket from a wooden cupboard near the stalls where we've settled Prince and Gypsy, and she helps me spread it on a mound of hay that will be my bed later.

"Ma don't like Pa's brother Ben very much and won't invite his family for supper anymore, no siree. Says they are ne'er-do-wells, always asking Pa for money. Money we can't spare."

After we get a place all squared away for me to spend the night, Eudora helps me shovel some grain from the feed room into the troughs in Prince and Gypsy's stalls. Ellie plays with a couple of the barn kittens. She's the youngest sister, I figure around my little brother Alvin's age. After I close the door to the feed room and latch it tight, I turn around and notice Ellie is staring at me like a barn owl with her huge eyes. "Why are you wearing those strange looking clothes?" she asks.

"My friend's mother made them for me while I was living with him."

"Was your friend Dakota? There's lots of Dakota people around here." Ellie's eyes get even bigger and rounder so that it's hard to look at anything but their blue watery centres. "What was it like to live with them? Did you smoke a peyote pipe or eat dog meat or sleep in a tipi? Did you understand their language?"

"They were Sisseton-Wahpeton, but they spoke the Dakota language. They also spoke English as good as you and I do. And they didn't live in a tipi; they lived in a house like yours over there." I jerk my head towards the black-and-white Schmidt house perched at the top of a rise on the prairie.

"I didn't eat dog, but I ate porcupine and bear and squirrel, and it was awful good. And I never smoked a pipe although my friend Joe's great-grandpa did. But his pipe had regular tobacco in it, I reckon, at least from the smell of it."

As we march up to the house four abreast, Ettie says, "Some of my friends at school say the Dakota aren't very clean."

"I was the dirty one when I arrived," I say. "I'd had an accident and the Little Thunder family doctored me back to health in a nice clean bed."

"Honest?" says Eudora with surprise in her voice.

"Cross my heart and hope to die, stick a needle in my eye."

"You know that rhyme in Kansas too?" Ellie asks. "We girls skip to it at school."

"Yeah, I know it, although Mama doesn't like me to say it at home. My brother Herman died a while back, so people talking about wanting to die gets her mighty upset."

"Your brother died?"

"How come?"

"How old was he?"

"Do you miss him?"

"Where's he buried?"

"Do you have other brothers and sisters?"

The questions tumble out of Ettie, Eudora, and Ellie's mouths quicker than a smattering of bullets. I tell them about Herman and Sylvester and Levi and Alvin. The Schmidt sisters heard the story about me getting left behind by the train when I explained it to their mother in the store. Now they've got a million questions about what's happened to me since Mr. Little Thunder found me, and I try to answer them as best I can.

I'm ready to have a little peace and quiet by the time we cross the porch into their house, but a tiny woman opens the front door and says in a voice much bigger than she is, "You just come straight into the kitchen, young man, and have a ham sandwich and a cold glass of buttermilk. Mrs. Schmidt sent word from the store you'd be arriving and I was to feed you and the girls."

"This is Violet," Eudora does the introduction. "She's our housekeeper and she looks after us sometimes when Ma and Pa are at work. Violet's the best cook in five counties, and if you treat her real polite she might give you a piece of her quince pie later, which is so good, you'll think you've died and gone to heaven."

"Eudora!" Ettie gives her a frosty glare.

"Oh, sorry," says Eudora putting her hand up to her mouth. "That maybe wasn't too polite seeing as your brother's just gone and died and all."

"Don't worry about it," I say. "He actually passed a while back." I realize as I say it that it's been near to eight months since Herman died. So much has happened to me in the last while, I scarce can believe I am the same boy who helped to dig my brother's grave in the cold and snow.

After my stomach is round and full of quince pie and buttermilk, Ettie, Eudora, and Ellie say they'll take me over to the mill to meet their pa.

Mr. Schmidt's red face wrinkles into a smile when the girls tell him who I am and how I've come to be in Sisseton. Mr. Schmidt pulls the heavy glove off his right hand to shake mine. "Of course I know your folks," he says. "Your grandma Marie was my mother's cousin once removed."

"I never knew Grandma Marie," I say, "but my grandpa is still living in Newton."

"Always meant to make a trip someday to visit those kinfolk in Kansas, but with the mill and the millinery and all, we've never made it. Ettie and Eudora, you'd better get back to the store to help your Ma, and Ellie, you go back to the house and help Violet fix supper. Peter can stay here and give me a hand."

I spend the next few hours in the mill. Mr. Schmidt shows me the giant millstones his grandfather had made in Germany and brought to South Dakota by ship and train.

"There have been millwrights in my family for more than a hundred years," Mr. Schmidt says proudly. "My grandfather started building this mill almost as soon as he arrived in America. My father taught my brother Ben and me all about milling but decided before he died I should be the one to run it. Ben wasn't too happy about that."

Five customers come to the mill to pick up wheat they've had ground into flour, and I help Mr. Schmidt carry the full sacks out to their wagons. He shows me how to throw the sack onto my back. "In the old days fellows who worked in flour mills were called sack and back boys," he tells me.

While he's readying the grindstones for a wagonload of wheat brought in by another customer, he asks me to empty the rat and mousetraps in the mill.

"Should be forty or so traps, Peter, here and there. Be right careful when you take out the dead varmints. Don't let a near dead one bite your finger or let the trap snap back on your hand."

I spend the next hour releasing dead creatures from the thirty-five traps I manage to find and dropping them into a pail Mr. Schmidt has given me. He's told me to throw the bodies into the cornfield behind the mill. I almost choke looking down at that heaping pile of dead rodents, some of them still warm, before I toss them between the corn stalks.

When I turn back for a minute, I see a flock of crows circling down ready to eat the bodies I've left. I can't help thinking about my gopher family. Where are they? Are they safe and getting fat and furry for winter, or did someone trap them or shoot them? Did the little ones become a crow's dinner?

Before we head home, Mr. Schmidt takes me next door to see his blacksmith shop. "Milling keeps me busy during summer and fall," he says, "but in winter and spring, I fix wagon wheels and shoe horses and sharpen knives and plows." Mr. Schmidt sure is a hard worker. He reminds me of my Papa who, besides farming our land, does carpentry work for other people and a little horse doctoring.

Violet outdoes herself at supper with fried chicken and sweet potatoes with gravy, cooked carrots, and a peach cobbler for dessert.

After supper Mrs. Schmidt lights the kerosene lamps and we stay sitting around the table while Mr. Schmidt reads from the Bible. The story is about Joseph and his brothers. Joseph had plenty of troubles—just like I've been having—but he stayed hopeful and believed things would get better. The people in Joseph's family got separated for a long spell, but in the end they were all together. Maybe next week I will be together with my family too.

After closing his Bible, Mr. Schmidt prays a real long time about everything from Mrs. Schmidt's gout to President Roosevelt's spot of trouble with the Japanese, and then we say good night. Mrs. Schmidt gives me one of the kerosene lamps to carry out to the barn and warns me to make sure I blow it out before I go to sleep.

I look up on my way across the yard and notice the autumn moon is not quite as full as it was the night Joe and I had our adventure in Sica Hollow.

Only two more moonlit nights and I might just be on a train to Minneapolis, and from there, back to my family.

I climb up to the hayloft, settle in under my blankets, blow out the lamp, and close my eyes.

Chapter 11

A FRIGHTENING CHOIR OF ANIMAL sounds wakes me. Prince and Gypsy are snorting, cows bellow, the rooster croaks, chickens squawk, and the pigs are barking. I jerk upright and throw off my blanket. The hayloft is hotter than Hades. I take a breath, burning my lungs and throat. I cough and sniff the smoky air.

Luckily I've slept in my clothes, so after I find my moccasins and feel for Herman's watch in my pocket, I start inching my way over to where I remember the hayloft ladder was. Something tells me it wouldn't be a good idea to light the kerosene lamp, but moonlight streaming in through tiny cracks in the barn roof and walls makes it just possible for me to see where I am going in the haze all around. I climb down the ladder as fast as I can.

The animal noises are getting so loud I might go deaf. The cats have joined in too and are yowling and snarling and hissing. I jump down from the last rung and turn around.

Lord have mercy! The barn's on fire! There's a crackling sound coming from the feed room that gets louder as I walk towards it. Smoke is billowing out from under the door, and when I touch the latch it burns my hand. I jump back. I need to get the animals out of the barn.

I make my way over to the big front door, and although it's dark, I figure out how to open it because it works just the same as the doors on my train car did. I lift the heavy hook out of the iron loop and push with all my might. The door slides open and the kittens and chickens and rooster scurry outside.

I hook my fingers into the corners of my mouth and whistle loud as ever I can. Prince and Gypsy and the Schmidts' four horses back out of their stalls and gallop out the door. They stop near the wagon that Mr. Schmidt left out of the barn so it would be ready to hitch up for church in the morning.

I wonder why the pigs and cows aren't coming, but then I remember there is a latched gate on the pigpen and the cows are tied up in their stalls. I crook my arm around my nose and head back into the barn. I know there are three cows because this morning the Schmidt sisters each introduced one to me: Clarabelle, Annabelle, and Lulubelle. Their stalls are side by side. The poor girls are in a horrible state, bawling and stomping, and they each land a few good kicks on my legs and shins as I slide past them to get to the ropes that hold them in place. Luckily the knots are easy to undo, especially with all my practising of Grandpa's puzzles, and it isn't long before the three belles are headed out of the barn.

I manage to open the pigpen gate, and in their rush to get outside the squealers knock me down face first. My head hits the barn floor hard and for a minute, I lay there winded. Then I feel something nudging me in the back. I look up. Gypsy has come back into the barn and she is pushing her nose real hard into my buckskin jacket and nickering loudly. Gypsy kneels down so I can crawl on her back. She carries me outside and canters towards the Schmidt house.

Just then, there is a loud whooshing sound that nearly jolts me off Gypsy's back. I jump down and turn around. The whole barn is engulfed in flames. Mr. and Mrs. Schmidt, Violet, and the three girls come stumbling out onto the porch of the house in their nightgowns. Mr. Schmidt is carrying the kerosene lamp. "Peter!" he shouts in a panicked voice, lifting the lamp high. "Peter, are you there?"

"Over here, sir," I say.

"Thanks be!" Mrs. Schmidt shouts. "Henry, we need to dig a trough around the barn so the fire can't spread to the house. The plow would come in handy, but it's in the barn. Eudora, run and get the hoes and spades from the back shed near the garden. Ellie, you bring out every pail and pot you can find in the house and start filling them with water from the slough. Ettie and Violet, find all the blankets and sheets and such, wet them at the pump, and start spreading them on the porch and around the house."

Mr. Schmidt strides over to me. "How are you, son?"

"Just fine, sir," I say strong as I can. "My lungs still ache some from taking in all that smoke while I was fetching the animals, but each breath is feeling a little better."

"We're much obliged to you, Peter, for saving the stock, but now we need to dig this trench around the barn. Think you can help me?"

"I surely can," I say.

Eudora is headed our way, dragging a couple of hoes in one hand and two spades in another. She hands them to us and we get started on a trench around the barn.

Minutes later we hear horse hooves, and two neighbours who have seen the blaze gallop into the yard. Without even a word, they pick up the pails Ellie has set out and head for the slough. They start filling the trench we are digging with water.

"There's no use trying to put water on that barn fire," says one of the men. "It's bigger than an elephant. All we can do is try and stop it from stomping across the yard to the house and hope it burns itself out."

Our trench is getting longer and deeper. We are digging like the blazes. My arms ache almost as much as my lungs.

I look up and see Mrs. Schmidt has a scythe in hand and is swathing down the tall grasses a ways behind the barn. I know she is worried the fire might jump from the grasses to the corn and wheat fields and they would lose their crop. The only good thing about the fire is that it has lit up the night sky so it is easy to see what we're doing.

Just when I'm wondering if we few humans are going to be able to stop the fire monster, we get a miracle—a true and mighty miracle. It starts to rain. I feel the first drop on my sweat-soaked head and then another on my neck and then another on my ear and then another and another. Eudora drops the tablecloth she is wetting at the pump and shrieks, "It's raining!"

We stop digging. Ellie and the men, heading up from the slough towards the barn with full pails of water, stop dead in their tracks and turn their faces to the sky. Raindrops splash onto their noses and into their mouths.

"Praise God!" Mrs. Schmidt shouts as she lifts one hand heavenward.

Soon it is pouring. The fire in the barn starts to smoke and sizzle. Mr. Schmidt stands with his hands still on his spade and his head bowed. His shoulders shake. I think he's crying.

Mrs. Schmidt comes over, dragging her scythe. She drops it and puts a hand on her husband's shoulder. He circles Mrs. Schmidt's waist with his arms. They stand forehead to forehead holding each other. It brings to mind how Papa held Mama at Herman's graveside. I wish Pastor Bartel were here now to say a little prayer of thanksgiving.

The two neighbours come over, and Mr. and Mrs. Schmidt shake their hands and thank them for their help before they mount their horses to ride off. "After church tomorrow we'll have a meeting to see about a barn raising for you," one of the men says.

"Let's go inside and get dry," says Mrs. Schmidt. "We can check out the damage tomorrow."

Violet makes hot cocoa and puts it out in cups on the kitchen table along with some of her quince pie, but we're all too shook up and exhausted to eat or drink much.

"I'm afraid I've got no blankets left, Peter. We wet them all during the fire, but I've put a nice soft pillow on the divan in the parlour for you," Violet tells me.

She ushers me into the parlour and I curl up on the divan, but it's too short for me, and a mite hard. After tossing and turning for a time, I slip down onto the horsehair rug on the floor, slide the pillow under my head, and close my eyes.

Chapter 12

IT CAN'T BE. I WAKE to the smell of smoke again. I jerk upright on the horsehair rug where I've spent the night. I sniff. The smoke seems to be coming from the kitchen. I scramble up to investigate. Violet is at the stove, frying eggs. She looks ever so smart in a navy blue dress she's covered with a big white apron. Ellie, Eudora, and Ettie are all sitting around the table. Mrs. Schmidt is poking curling tongs into the kerosene lamp to heat them and is crimping Ettie's hair. Ellie and Eudora already have curls springing round their heads

"There you are, Peter," says Mrs. Schmidt, spying me.

"I thought I smelled smoke again," I say.

"No need to worry," Mrs. Schmidt replies. "Just kept the curling iron in Ellie's hair a little too long and singed it some. She'll be fine."

"That happens to Mama too sometimes when she curls her hair," I say.

Mrs. Schmidt finishes Ettie's hair, ties her curls up with a gingham bow. "Violet's making you children some eggs and fried bread. Once you've had that you need to get ready for church."

"I kind of figured after last night's excitement we wouldn't be going to church this morning." I say.

Mrs. Schmidt looks shocked. "Goodness me, Peter! After what the good Lord did for us last night sending that rain shower, going to service and thanking him is the least we can do."

Violet puts a platter of fried eggs on the table.

"Go on and eat, children, and then, Peter, you can wash up at the basin on the back porch. I've left some old Sunday meeting clothes of Henry's there for you to wear. Violet got up early this morning and shortened the pant legs and shirt sleeves some. Should fit you just fine. Cinch your waist with the leather belt I found. You can't go to church in your buckskin clothes. They reek of smoke from the fire. Violet will clean them for you."

Mr. Schmidt comes in as I'm washing up on the porch. He walks right by me into the kitchen as if he doesn't even notice I'm there. His face is white and his moustache is quivering.

"Why, Henry, you look like you've seen a ghost," Mrs. Schmidt says as her husband slides down onto a chair. "What is it? What's happened?"

"You know how Peter helped me get all the animals in the corral last night? Well, after I'd fed and watered them best I could this morning and hitched up the horses to the wagon for going to church, I thought I'd just poke around in the ashes of the barn a bit to see if I could find any clues as to how the fire got started."

"And did you find anything?" Mrs. Schmidt asks.

Mr. Schmidt's voice cracks and quavers. "Yes, I did. I found a body. I found a skeleton in the ashes. There's a dead person out there in our barn."

"Do you know who it is?" I ask coming in from the back porch where I've overheard everything.

"No idea, Peter. The clothes have all been burned, and the hair too, so I can't really tell even if it was a man or woman."

"What are we going to do, Papa?" asks Eudora.

"I'll speak with Sheriff Stevens directly after the church service. Maybe he can ride out here and take a look and tell us what we ought to do."

"Don't forget they were going to have a meeting about a barn raising for us after the service, Henry," says Mrs. Schmidt.

"Yes. I know."

Mr. Schmidt points to a stack of thick ledgers teetering on the table. "I couldn't sleep last night. I was toting up the accounts for the mill and the millinery over and over, trying to figure out where we can find some extra dollars to buy enough wood from the sawmill to rebuild the barn. It could start snowing in a month's time and we'll need a place for the animals."

"Perhaps we should build in a different place," says Mrs. Schmidt. "What with a dead person in the barn and all, the old spot might just be haunted."

After my night in Sica Hollow with Joe, I'd be the last one to discount the presence of ghosts or spirits, but Mr. Schmidt doesn't agree with me or his wife.

"Now don't you talk crazy, Euphemia. You'll scare the children. First things first. We need to find out who the poor person is lying dead and charred black as night in our barn, and I want to know whether or not they started the fire. Maybe the sheriff can help us find out who it is."

The ride to church is strangely quiet. Even the Schmidt girls, who usually jabber on non-stop, hardly say a word. I suspect we are all tired from last night's adventures and all wondering about that dead body in the barn. We stop at Violet's church to let her off and then continue on into town.

As we pull into the churchyard, everyone is circling around talking excitedly and the church bells are ringing.

A man strides over to our wagon before we can even get out. He is holding a Bible and wearing a white shirt and a black suit coat.

"Morning, Pastor Kraybill," Mrs. Schmidt says.

"Morning, Euphemia. Morning, Henry. Heard you had quite the night at your place. So sorry to hear about the barn, but glad you are all safe."

"Thanks, Pastor," says Mr. Schmidt.

"Now I hate to add to your troubles with some more bad news, but it seems as if your brother Ben has gone and disappeared, Henry. Your sister-in-law Martha went to see Sheriff Stevens this morning. Ben's not been home in three days and she's mighty worried. Sheriff's brought Martha to church and has let everyone know he's going to mount a search party directly after the service."

"Pastor, we all know Ben can drink more liquor than he should and he sometimes wanders off," says Mrs. Schmidt.

"But he's never been gone this long before," says a man striding up to us. He is wearing a gun belt and has a silver star on his vest. I guess this must be the sheriff.

Just then, Mrs. Schmidt gasps in a horrified sort of way. She covers her mouth with her hand. She looks at Mr. Schmidt and Mr. Schmidt looks back at her.

"That search party may not be necessary, Sheriff," Mr. Schmidt says. "I think I might just know where my brother Ben is."

Chapter 13

THE CHURCH SERVICE SEEMS TO last forever. I was sure when Mr. and Mrs. Schmidt shared their suspicion that the dead body in their barn might be Mr. Schmidt's brother Ben we'd all head right on back to the farm. But no such thing!

"The body will still be there after the service," the sheriff comments. "And we might need a little divine help getting to the bottom of things. Won't hurt for you to stay here for some praying and singing. I'll be waiting right outside."

"I agree," Pastor Kraybill says. "Henry, I'll meet with everyone after the service about a barn raising for you come next Saturday. The snow could fly any day now. You never know. And those animals of yours need to be sheltered."

"Thanks, Pastor Kraybill," Mr. Schmidt says. "I'll order the lumber for the barn first thing Monday morning before I open the mill."

"Do you need us to have a special offering this morning to help you pay for that lumber?"

"No, thank you, Pastor," says Mr. Schmidt clearing his throat and adjusting his bow tie. "I think we can manage, but you might want to think of taking up a collection for Martha and the kids. If Ben is really and truly gone, they are going to be suffering some."

Mrs. Schmidt lays her hand gentle-like on Mr. Schmidt's arm and says softly, "It's not like you haven't helped them out plenty in the past, Henry. You did your best. You know Ben wasted most of the profits from his farm, and that's why his family is in the poor house the way they are. Your father did the right thing leaving you the mill. Ben just couldn't have handled it."

Mr. Schmidt puts his hand over his wife's. "Now, Euphemia, there's no good comes speaking ill of the dead."

"We don't know for sure he is dead," Mrs. Schmidt says. "Maybe the man in the barn is someone else."

I sit between Ettie and Eudora during the service, but it is hard for anyone to really listen to the pastor because Martha, Ben's wife, is sobbing the whole time. Quiet-like, mind you, but still everyone can hear her.

Her two sons sit on either side of her. They seem a little older than me and they look straight ahead, their faces as empty as the blackboard at the end of the school day. They don't even seem to notice their mother is crying.

I'm not sure I could sit still in a church service if I thought my Papa was dead, but then my Papa is hardworking and has always looked after our family, and the only time he takes a drink is to have a glass of Grandpa's homemade wine at Christmas. Would you still love a parent that drank too much and couldn't put food on the table or keep a job? I suspect you would, but I reckon it might be harder than loving a parent who took care of their family proper.

Growing up in Newton, I don't recall anyone's father being like that. But maybe some of those men I saw going into the saloon in Omaha were not doing right by their families because they liked to drink and gamble more than was good for them. Maybe that's why Pastor Bartel back home talked about saloons as dens of sin.

Thinking about Omaha reminds me of Annie and how her Papa rescued us and all those other people from the broken roller coaster. Would my Papa have climbed fearlessly into the air like that to save me? Or would he have jumped into Enemy Swim Lake to help a stranger the way Mr. Little Thunder did? I think he would have.

There are lots of different kinds of people in the world. Makes me wonder what kind of grownup I might be someday. In *Captains Courageous,* Harvey turns out to be a real different person because of his unexpected adventure. Will that happen to me too? At any rate, this adventure of mine is surely making me ask lots of questions that never even entered my brain before.

During the church service we sing "Amazing Grace" and "We're Marching to Zion," and during the offering "Mine Eyes Have Seen the Glory," and if I close my eyes I can hear Mama's voice soaring up high on those hallelujahs.

I wonder if she is singing right now, in a church in Saskatchewan?

Has my Papa started building our sod house yet, or have he and Sylvester and Levi gone off to look for me?

Is little Alvin missing me? Does he ask Mama, "Where's Peter?"

Has Mama written a letter to Grandpa back home in Newton to tell him I've gone missing?

The sheriff follows our wagon home. One of his deputies is riding with him, and we've taken the girls' cousins—Ben's sons, Orrin and Leander—along with us. The distance between the church and the Schmidt house seems twice as long this time and we drive in a silence only interrupted by Mr. Schmidt clearing his throat regularly as if he might be getting ready to say something.

It starts to rain again right after we pick up Violet from her church, and it isn't long before we are soaked and shivering. As we pull into the Schmidt's yard, the downpour suddenly stops.

"Girls, you come inside with me and Violet and set the table for lunch," says Mrs. Schmidt as I offer my hand to Ettie, Eudora, and Ellie to help them out of the wagon. "Nice to see your mother's raised you to be a gentleman," Mrs. Schmidt says to me.

The menfolk all head towards the barn. Halfway across the yard, Orrin shouts, "Look over there." He's spotted something caught in the tall grasses Mrs. Schmidt left off cutting down when the rain started last night. Orrin strides over and plucks a piece of white cloth from the browning sheaves. "This here is my father's." He walks back and shows us a large blue S embroidered in the corner of a dirty handkerchief spattered with snot that's gone running again in the rain. "Ma gave it to Pa last Christmas."

We all study the handkerchief as if it might be able to speak to us.

"Henry, when's the last time you saw Ben?" the sheriff asks.

"Yesterday," says Mr. Schmidt. "He came by the mill in the morning."

"What did he want?"

"Wanted me to lend him some money."

"And did you?"

"No. I didn't."

"And what happened then?"

"Ben stalked off without another word to me. I felt real bad. He's my brother and Pa left me everything. I helped Ben buy his farm after Pa died, but he just hasn't made a go of it and I can't keep lending him money. Times haven't been easy for us lately either."

"Well, let's go take a look in the barn," says the sheriff.

I'm not sure I want to go, but everyone seems to be expecting me to follow so I do. The last dead body I saw was my brother Herman's, and he was frozen solid cause it was February and we'd kept him out in the summer kitchen till we buried him. Now I'm going to see a body that's been burned to the bone. I'm not sure I'm ready for that.

The rain has made a mess of things, and we pick our way through the ashy muck that covers what was once the dirt floor of the old barn. When we reach the spot where the feed room used to be, we see the skeleton. It has no skin on it at all and the bones are a kind of grey colour. I feel like throwing up, but I swallow hard and stand my ground.

Orrin inhales a sob, turns around and strides away back to the wagon. No wonder. Imagine looking at the burned skeleton of what might be your father. But Leander walks slow and steady over to the body and hunkers down beside it. He looks carefully at the skull and then reaches out and ever so gently touches one of the teeth.

"Hi there, Pa," he whispers. "You rest easy now."

Leander stands up. "This is my Pa. His one front tooth is broken off, kind of jagged-like. Happened when he got in a fight with a wanderer he owed some money to. I went to the wanderer camp to fetch him after they sent one of their kids to our place. Pa was pretty beat up after the fight and his tooth was broke."

The sheriff clears his throat. "Mighty sorry for your loss, son. You have any idea what your Pa was doing here? He was a smoking man, weren't he? Could he have started the fire by accident with some burning tobacco from his pipe? Or, Henry, do you think he was angry enough to start a fire on purpose?"

Mr. Schmidt puts a hand on Leander's shoulder. "Sheriff, I don't think I need to know. What's done is done. Whether the fire was set on purpose or it was an accident don't make no never mind now. I need to bury my brother and build a new barn. If you don't mind taking my nephews home, Peter and I will load up the body on my wagon and bring it into town. I'll arrange with Pastor Kraybill to have a service, maybe Wednesday. Leander, tell your mother I'll come over to talk to her directly after I've left your Pa's body at the undertaker."

After the sheriff and the others have left, I help Mr. Schmidt wrap the body in some blankets I fetch from the house. We tie rope round and round the blankets and then carefully place the body in the back of the wagon.

In town, I help Mr. Schmidt unload the body at the undertaker's and I wait in the churchyard while Mr. Schmidt talks with the pastor. At his brother Ben's house, I sit silently around the table with Leander and Orrin and their mother as plans are made for the funeral service and burial. I notice Mr. Schmidt takes two one-dollar bills from his pocket and tucks them under the Bible on the table before we leave.

It's funny. I thought this day might seem long as can be. Thought I'd wear my patience thin waiting for Monday morning to meet that train agent from Minneapolis and start my journey home. But the day has gone by mighty fast with all that's happened. Mr. Schmidt seems tuckered out after supper and suggests we go straight to bed. No Bible reading and prayers tonight.

"Say goodbye to the women now," he tells me. "You and I will head into town early. Don't want to take a chance on you missing that train agent."

Ellie, Eudora, and Ettie each shake my hand solemnly as they say goodbye before heading on up to bed.

Mrs. Schmidt shakes my hand too. "Thanks kindly for taking me in," I say.

She nods. "Wish your stay had been a little less exciting, Peter, but we are ever so grateful to you for saving all our stock last night."

I bed down again on the horsehair rug in the parlour. I'm not sure I'll be able to sleep I'm so excited about what the coming day will bring. But the next thing I know, Violet is shaking my shoulder and saying, "Coffee's ready and the potatoes are frying. Come on into the kitchen."

THE SKY IS JUST TURNING pink as Mr. Schmidt climbs up into the wagon and we head into town.

I am riding Gypsy and Prince follows the wagon. I turn around and take one more gander at the burned barn, the animals in the corral, and the Schmidt house. I want to remember how things look so when I tell my family all about my adventures in South Dakota, it will seem real to them and help them understand everything that has happened to me.

Chapter 14

WE PULL UP TO THE train station, and sure enough that engine from Minneapolis is already there, black as the burned barn timbers, with smoke drifting out its stack. Attached to it is my very own train car, with the frayed end-piece of the rope I had tied to its door handle batting about in the morning breeze. It seems a lifetime ago that I left that car. Mr. Schmidt ties up his horses to the hitching post and hurries up to the engine. I think he is worried the train might leave without me. I am too.

"I'll be right back," I tell Prince and Gypsy before hightailing it after him.

Mr. Schmidt is talking to a man beside the tracks no taller than I am. His beard is white and scraggly. Round, steel-rimmed spectacles seem ready to slide off his nose. He's wearing a faded blue uniform with a dented rusty badge on the lapel. His oil-stained hat looks like it could belong to a soldier.

"This is Mr. Miller, Peter," Mr. Schmidt says as I reach the two men. "He's the train engineer, and I was just starting to tell him your story, but he seems to know all about you."

"Pleased to meet you, Mr. Miller."

His hand when I shake it is greasy and gritty, but despite that, his grip is sure.

"Had your breakfast, son?" he asks me first thing.

"Yes." I notice he's had his. Bits of bread and egg yolk are stuck in his beard.

"Well then, we should be off. Got word just before I left Minneapolis you'd be here. The company vice-president received a telegram from up there in Canada asking after your whereabouts. I've got orders to take you to Minneapolis with me and then hook up this car to the next train leaving for Humboldt, Saskatchewan. Appears that's the closest station to where your folks got their homestead and it's where your two brothers arrived some weeks back."

"Sounds just fine to me, sir," I say to Mr. Miller.

"I'll help the boy load his horses into the train car," Mr. Schmidt tells him.

"I put in some fresh straw and water for your horses," Mr. Miller reports. "Your father wired some funds for us to do that, but the company vice-president gave orders not to use your family's money. He feels real bad about your car coming uncoupled out there near Dakota territory, and says taking care of you and your horses is the least we can do."

Mr. Miller crawls up into the engine, and to my surprise, a man in blue overalls and a cap like

Mr. Miller's pokes his head out the window. "This here's my fireman. Name's Denver."

Denver points a quivering jaw in my direction and nods without looking me in the eye. "Denver don't say much, but he's a mighty fine fireman. He and I are going to get the boiler hot as we can while you square those horses of yours away."

Mr. Schmidt helps me lead Prince and Gypsy into the boxcar, and together we lift the slanted board that makes a walkway between the tracks and the train for them. We shove the heavy board up and into the boxcar. I remember it took me near to a whole morning to drag that board in place when I was all alone and hurt and needed to get Prince and Gypsy out into the fresh air. What a difference now with Mr. Schmidt's strong arms to help, and me all sturdy and healed up thanks to the Little Thunders' doctoring and Violet's cooking.

Mr. Schmidt shakes my hand hard and sure just the way Papa did when I left Newton, like I'm a real man. Sometimes I think about what a little boy I was the day I left home all excited but with no idea about what was to happen to me. But now I feel a heap more grown up.

After all, I've killed a copperhead and climbed down a roller coaster. I crawled back up after a terrible fall down a ravine and survived a near drowning. I rescued my friend from quicksand and saved a barn full of animals from a fire. What with all my adventures, I'm becoming more and more brave and grown up, like Harvey was at the end of *Captains Courageous*. Will Mama and Papa and my brothers even recognize me?

"It's not a long trip, Peter," Mr. Schmidt says, bringing my head back from its meanderings. "You should be in Minneapolis this afternoon. Greet your folks for me and tell them someday I just might come for a visit. Never been to Canada. Might be I want to see another country in this world before I die."

Mr. Schmidt begins to slide the door in place. "Goodbye," I say trying to sound manly and sure of myself.

"*Gruss Gott*, Peter," I hear Mr. Schmidt say just before the door clangs shut. The familiar phrase almost brings a tear to my eye. I stand between Prince and Gypsy and put one hand on each horse. "We're going home," I say.

I'm all at sixes and sevens as the train speeds down the tracks to Minneapolis. I find the puzzle from Grandpa that I've left behind in the boxcar, but after only ten minutes—according to my brother Herman's pocket watch—I figure it out and the four sections of the puzzle slide apart. I tried to solve that puzzle all the way from Newton to Omaha without any luck, and now for some reason I can see the way to untwist the metal pieces clear as can be.

To make the time go by, I sing a few of Mama's favourite songs—"Let Me Call You Sweetheart" and "Down by the Old Mill Stream"—and even some of the hymns Grandpa takes a shine to, like "A Mighty Fortress" and "Bringing in the Sheaves." Gypsy and Prince don't seem to like my singing much; they paw and snort a bunch, so I stop after a time. I eat the lunch Violet sent along with me and I drop off for a snooze with a piece of her juicy quince pie sticky in my hand.

I'm awake, though, when the train screeches to a stop and Denver the fireman comes to open the door. I peer out and Denver jerks his head and his thumb towards the train station.

Some men are already helping Mr. Miller unhook my boxcar, and the engineer looks up and says, "Welcome to Minneapolis, Peter. We're going to get your car coupled up with the train heading to Humboldt, Saskatchewan, in the morning. Don't you worry a mite about your horses here. I'll look to them. You go on into the station and find the ticket agent. Name's Harold Larsen. He's going to get you taken care of for the night."

I give Prince and Gypsy a pat and whisper that I'll be back, and then I walk into the station and just stand there staring. I don't think I have ever been in a building so big. I could skate across the shiny marble floors. I look way up at the arching pale-blue ceiling.

The afternoon sun is streaming in through huge, high windows and warming the hundreds of people in the station who are rushing around like an army of ants, but not as organized as ants, who always march in straight lines. These folks dart about criss-crossing and dodging and sometimes bumping into each other. The noisy crowd reminds me of the Omaha amusement park where I had my first roller coaster ride with Annie. I spy a barred window with the word "tickets" in big letters above it. I wait in the long line in front of it until it is finally my turn. "I'm Peter Schmidt," I say, introducing myself to a man in a white shirt and checkered vest behind the window. "Are you Mr. Larsen?"

"Yes, I am," says Mr. Larsen, smiling so big and wide that all his square white teeth show and the ends of his curling moustache almost touch his cheeks.

"I know all about you, Peter Schmidt, and I've been expecting you. Mr. James Olsen himself, the Great Western Railway vice-president here in Minneapolis, wishes me to convey his deepest regrets about your train car being left behind near Sisseton. In order to make it up to you, he has personally arranged for you to spend the night in the West Hotel at his expense."

Mr. Larsen hollers, "Samson!" and a boy about my age pokes his head round a door behind the ticket agent.

"Samson, this is Peter Schmidt. I want you to walk over to the West Hotel with him and make sure he gets checked in at the front desk. Just tell them he's Mr. Olsen's guest. They will know what to do."

I follow Samson out of the station and he finds a path through the maze of carriages and horses standing in front of the grand brick building's front entrance.

As we walk down the street side by side, Samson begins to whistle. "I don't know that song," I say.

"It's called 'Come Take a Trip in My Airship.'"

"My family likes music, but I've never heard that one," I tell him.

"It's pretty new. Miss Ginger, one of the entertainers in the dining room at the West Hotel, has been singing it lately. I often have to take passengers to and from the hotel and sometimes when I'm waiting in the lobby for folks I can hear Miss Ginger singing. She's got a voice can make your worries fly away."

"Why would she be singing about an airship? What's that?"

"You haven't heard of them?"

"Can't say that I have. I saw some hot-air balloons at an amusement park in Omaha. Is that the same thing?"

"I guess in a way, but these are real airships that carry lots of passengers. They've been experimenting with them over in Europe—France, mostly. This one fella earned a whole pile of money for flying his airship around the Eiffel Tower."

"And how do you know about airships, Samson?"

"I read newspapers. Passengers leave them in the station all the time. I had to quit school after my pa died to help provide for my ma and three little sisters, but I can still learn stuff from reading the papers."

I shake my head. The world is a bigger place with more stuff going on than I ever imagined. I wonder if maybe I will have a chance to go to Europe someday and see things like the Eiffel Tower and maybe even fly in an airship.

Chapter 15

"WELL, HERE WE ARE," SAYS Samson stopping in front of a towering building with pillars like the ones on ancient temples.

"This is the West Hotel. It is here on the corner of Fifth Street and Hennepin Avenue. And if you walk down Hennepin you get back to the train station."

I wait in the lobby while Samson goes up to the front desk. I stare at all the people in their fine clothes. There are ladies in long silk dresses with flowing skirts and tight jackets closed up with dozens of little pearl buttons. Many are carrying umbrellas and wearing huge hats with feathers and fruit and flowers on them. Why are they carrying umbrellas when it's not even close to looking like rain, and how do they keep those hats balanced on their heads? How would Mama look in a hat like that?

Many of the men have tall, shiny black hats that look like the pipe on Mama's stove. They are dressed in black suits with long jackets that have tails flying out the back. Some of the men are carrying canes like the one Grandpa uses, but they are way too young to need a cane to walk.

Samson comes over with a boy dressed in an outfit that looks a mite like a Union Army uniform. There are dozens of shiny buttons down the front and a funny hat that brings to mind a round cake. It looks like it would slide off the boy's head if it weren't held in place by an elastic band that goes round his chin.

"Meet Danny," says Samson. "He's the bellhop and will take you to your room. Good luck, Peter. Nice to meet you."

Samson strides off before I get a chance to even say goodbye. I hear him whistling that airship song as he hurries out of the hotel.

I follow Danny up to a pair of wooden doors with fancy iron grating across the front. He pushes apart the grating first and then slides open the doors before stepping inside a huge box with beautiful carvings all over walls.

"Come on," he says, beckoning me into the box.

"What is that?" I ask, staying right where I am.

"It's an elevator," Danny replies. "Haven't you ever been on one before?"

"No sirree," I reply. "I haven't even ever heard of an elevator."

"Well, it's a kind of moving box," says Danny, "that will take us up to the fourth floor of the hotel where your room is."

"Is it safe?" I ask.

"Not everyone thinks so," Danny replies. "But I've been on it hundreds of times and nothing has ever happened to me."

I walk inside with careful steps.

"Hold up there!" A man in a white suit who has a white bushy moustache and plenty of white curly hair slips into the elevator.

"What floor, sir?" Danny asks him politely.

"Third, please."

Danny closes the doors and turns a shiny brass handle on the wall. The elevator begins to move up. It feels funny. My stomach seems to drop as the elevator rises.

I must look uncomfortable because the man in the white suit asks, "First time on an elevator, son?"

"Yes, sir," I reply.

Just then the elevator makes a groaning sound, gives a lurch, and comes to a stop. The man in the white suit topples over and lands on the floor with a thud. I reach out a hand to help him up.

"Are you all right, sir?" Danny asks as the man brushes some dirt off the arms of his jacket.

"No harm done, son. Let's see if you can get this contraption started again."

Danny tries turning the handle. Nothing happens.

"What do we do now?" I ask.

"Just wait," Danny says with a sigh. "This happens at least once a week. Someone will soon realize the elevator has stopped and will get Mr. Harmer, the engineer. He's friends with every little moving part in this elevator and he can always get it going again."

Danny starts to whistle. I tap my foot, and the man in the white suit combs his moustache with his fingers.

After a time, he says kindly, "I'm from Connecticut, son. Where are you from?"

"Now that's sort of hard to say, sir," I reply. "You see I was from Newton, Kansas, but my family is moving up to Canada to a place called Drake, Saskatchewan."

"Yet I find you without your family in a stuck elevator in the finest hotel in Minneapolis. Why's that?"

"Well, sir," I say. "That's a long story."

"Stories are my specialty and it seems we need to pass some time," the man remarks. "I'd be obliged if you would tell me yours."

The man looks so interested I begin telling him about the morning Papa and Mama said goodbye to me at the train station in Kansas. By the time I have finished describing how I killed the copperhead and saved the gophers, Danny has turned around and I can tell he is listening real careful to everything I'm saying. The older gentleman keeps saying "ah" in a short humming sort of way whenever I finish a sentence or two.

I am just at the part where Annie and I are being rescued from the roller coaster in Omaha when the elevator groans and lurches and starts moving.

Danny turns around to put his hand back on the handle that moves the elevator up and down.

"I'm right sorry this thing started," he says. "Your story is awful exciting. Did you get off that roller coaster safe and sound?"

"Well, he's here, isn't he?" the man in the white suit says with a chuckle. "Guess you made it. But I still want to know how you got from Omaha to Minneapolis."

The elevator stops and Danny opens the door. "Third floor, sir."

The man starts walking forward and then turns around. "Are you spending the night here at the West Hotel?" he asks me.

"Yes, sir. I am."

"And who are you eating dinner with, young man?"

Danny speaks up. "Arrangements have been made for him to eat in the dining room, sir."

"And will he be eating alone?"

"As far as I know, sir," says Danny.

"What's your name, son?" the man demands, looking me right in the eye.

"Peter Schmidt, sir."

"Well, Peter Schmidt, I'd be obliged if you joined me in the dining room for supper tonight. Shall we say around 6:30? If I'm not there just ask the waiter to seat you at Samuel Clemens's table."

As Mr. Clemens starts ambling down the hallway, Danny closes the elevator doors.

"Lucky you, having dinner with Samuel Clemens," he says.

"Why? Is he famous or something?" I ask.

"Famous?" Danny chuckles. "That man is one of America's greatest authors. He's toured all over the country giving talks and lectures. On his book covers he uses a different name, Mark Twain. Haven't you ever heard of him?"

Chapter 16

I'M JUST A MITE JUMPY getting ready for dinner. Will I know how to behave in the company of a famous author in a fancy hotel dining room? Will I remember my manners? Mama's voice slices into my worry.

"Elbows off the table, Peter."

"Don't lick your knife, Peter."

"Close your mouth when you chew, Peter."

I'm going to have lots to remember during supper.

I have a good long soak in the claw-foot tub in the bathroom. It is almost deep enough to dive into. I can't believe how much hot water comes out of the tap. Back home in Kansas we only bathed on Saturday nights.

Mama and I would pull the big tin tub from the back porch into the kitchen. She and I would fill pails with water at the pump and pour them into a giant copper cauldron on top of the stove where the water heated. Then Mama and I would dip the hot water out of the cauldron into the tin tub.

Mama bathed first, then Alvin, then me, then Levi and Sylvester, and finally Papa. By the time Papa got his turn the water wasn't even warm anymore and awful dirty. But he never complained a bit and plopped into that tub as if he was a duck dipping into a pond.

I wish I could give Papa a chance to have a bath in this pearly white tub with gold taps and a never-ending supply of hot water. He'd think he'd died and gone to heaven.

When Danny showed me into the room earlier, he pointed out some clothing hanging in the closet. "I'm to tell you these are from Mr. Olsen, the vice-president of the Great Western Railroad Company. He's left a note for you on the night-stand." I decided to read it right away.

Dear Mr. Schmidt,

On behalf of the Great Western Railroad Company, I wish to extend my deepest regrets about the detachment of the railroad car carrying you and your horses. We have sent word to your parents and they will be awaiting your safe arrival at the Humboldt train station two days hence. Please accept a night in this hotel, some new clothing, and dinner in the dining room at our expense as a way of offering you and your family our most heartfelt apologies.

Wishing you a prosperous future in your new home in Canada, I remain

Yours most sincerely,

Mr. James Olsen

I tuck the letter into the nice, roomy carpetbag sitting on the bedclothes. The generous Mr. Olsen must have provided that too. I take out the starched white underwear and socks I find inside.

There are some blue dungarees and a plaid flannel shirt hanging in the closet. I figure I'll put them on tomorrow for the train trip. But on another hanger is a smart blue suit that looks like something a sailor would wear. It has tight pants with gold buttons down the sides of the legs. The shirt has a wide navy collar trimmed with white bands and fastened with a broad bow. There's even a pair of shiny black shoes with silver buckles. I feel a mite uncomfortable in the suit and wish I could just wear the buckskin clothes and moccasins Joe's mother made me.

But even though Violet washed them for me after the fire and they look good as new, they might not be proper for a fancy hotel dining room. My new shoes pinch my feet a mite, but the sailor suit hangs a little loose on my bones. When I look into the mirror above the bureau, I just stare for a long spell. I am so clean and dandy and citified, I hardly recognize myself. I seem to have grown some taller since I left Newton.

Danny whistles when I step into the elevator to go down to the dining room. "You sure clean up purty, Peter. You look like one fine gentleman."

As I leave the elevator, Danny points to the dining room door, guarded on either side by palm trees. "You'll find Mr. Clemens in there," he tells me.

Sure enough the author has already arrived and is puffing on the fattest cigar I've ever seen. His glass is brim full of whiskey, no doubt poured from the tall bottle standing on the table. He spots me as soon as I enter.

"Over here, Peter," he calls, beckoning me over.

I sit down in the high-backed chair across the snowy tablecloth from Mr. Clemens. A waiter pops up immediately and Mr. Clemens orders me something called a sarsaparilla. It tastes fizzy and fine.

"They're serving steaks and mashed potatoes with gravy tonight, Peter, so we are in luck." Mr. Clemens's voice is so loud and hearty that most of the other people in the dining room turn to stare at us.

"Minnesota beef is surely tasty. It's been my favourite meal here at the West Hotel on my previous visits."

While I sip my sarsaparilla, Mr. Clemens unbuckles a worn brown satchel and takes out a grey notebook and a thick black pencil. He picks up the steak knife by his plate and whittles the pencil's stubby lead tip to a sharp point.

"Now, Peter, I'd be obliged if you'd finish your story. When I had to disembark from the elevator you were just climbing down that roller coaster in Omaha. What did you and your young lady friend do when your feet first touched the ground?"

I cough a little, nervous-like, before launching into the next part of my story, and Mr. Clemens scribbles fast and furious in his notebook as I talk.

Whenever I stop to take a breath, Mr. Clemens puts down his pencil and takes a gulp of whiskey and a puff of his cigar. I've just told him about rescuing Joe from Sica Hollow when our food arrives.

Mr. Clemens puts up his hand to stop me, fills up his whiskey glass again and says, "We will commence with the rest of your story after we eat. This steak needs to be downed while it's hot and juicy."

I watch Mr. Clemens cut into his steak with the same knife that just sharpened his pencil and I pick up my knife to do likewise.

"Can I ask why you are writing down my story?" I venture as I make my mashed potatoes into a mountain and pour gravy down its sides.

"Well, I'm an author, Peter. Ever heard of my books? *The Adventures of Tom Sawyer*, *The Adventures of Huckleberry Finn*, or *The Prince and the Pauper*?"

"Can't say I have," I falter and my face flushes. "But my brother Herman had a shelf of books and he read a goodly number to me. My two favourites were *Captains Courageous* and *Robinson Crusoe*."

"Well, if you liked those, you'd probably like my stories too. They're about boys close to your age who have powerful adventures. And it seems to me you've been having quite a powerful adventure yourself, young Peter. Thought maybe I could use some of your excitement in my next book."

"You might write about me? Why, that would truly be an honour, sir. What's your next book going to be called?"

"Don't know yet. Fact is, I haven't written a book for a long spell, Peter."

"Why?"

Mr. Clemens takes another gulp of his whiskey. His voice is sad and slurry.

"I've had quite a burden of grief to carry of late, Peter. My sweetheart Livy, the light of my life, died not so long ago. And before her, my daughter Susie went to her grave from meningitis, and my son Langdon succumbed to diphtheria."

Tears trickle down Mr. Clemens's cheeks and soak into his bristly moustache hairs.

"My condolences," I say as soft and gentle as ever I can. "My family's had some sorrows too, sir," I confess. "The reason I was travelling with the horses was due to my big brother Herman's sudden death, and my little brother Alvin, well, he gets these shaking fits and we don't know why."

"Might be epilepsy," says Mr. Twain. "Ever heard of that?"

"Can't say that I have, sir."

"I have two daughters left and one of them, my girl Jean, has those shaking fits too. The doctors tell me it's called epilepsy."

"And how do the doctors try to heal her?" I ask, perhaps a little too eagerly. Wouldn't it be something if I could learn about a way to help my brother Alvin?

"There's not really much they can do, Peter. My dear Jean's heart is weak, and I worry she may not be long for this world either."

Mr. Clemens has stopped eating and is draining his whiskey glass in big gulps now. The waiter comes to take our near-empty plates away.

Mr. Clemens picks up his pencil and I notice it is trembling in his hand. He opens his notebook. His jaw twitches, his shoulders shake, and then BANG! His forehead lands smack dab down on the open notebook pages.

"Mr. Clemens," I say, getting up and reaching across the table. "Mr. Clemens." I shake his shoulder. He gives a loud snore. I do believe he's fallen asleep. I take his burning cigar out of his hand and place it on the spittoon near the table. Just then, the waiter appears with dishes of ice cream.

"I think my dinner companion may have taken ill," I say to the waiter.

"Just a bit too much whiskey, I surmise," the waiter whispers so the other diners can't hear. "It happens to him almost every night. I'll get the steward to escort Mr. Clemens out."

I help the steward take Mr. Clemens to his room. We lay him on the bed, and I carefully remove his shoes. He snorts and snuffles a few times but doesn't say a word.

When I return to the dining room, my ice cream has melted to a syrupy puddle in the dish. I'm tempted to just drink it up, but that wouldn't be mannerly, so I dip into it with a spoon. It is sweet and still cool.

Later when I'm in bed myself, I think about Mr. Clemens and how sadness in your life can sometimes sneak up and just take over things, kind of like it did for Mama after Herman died. I suspect Mama's gone from fretting over Herman now to fretting over me, her missing son. I hope when she sees me safe and sound I'll be able to put a smile back on her face.

I say a quick prayer for Mr. Clemens—that something will come into his life to bring him a little spot of joy again.

The next morning, Danny arrives at my door bright and early to take me down to the dining room for breakfast. He carries my carpetbag and gives it to the steward behind the front desk to watch while I eat my eggs and hash. When I go to retrieve it just before I leave for the train station, the steward hands me not only my carpetbag but a book as well.

"Mr. Clemens asked me to give this to you," he says.

I take the book. The cover says: *The Adventures of Tom Sawyer*, by Mark Twain. I open it and see Mr. Clemens has written something on the flyleaf.

My dear Peter,

Best wishes on your further adventures. I would like to apologize for my unseemly behavior last evening. I have been letting *life's sorrows drown me of late, but I am hoping to get my head above water shortly. I hope you will enjoy this book. The last line of the story is meant for you as well as my hero Tom.*

Samuel L. Clemens

I turn to the last page and read the last line: *So endeth this chronicle. It being strictly a history of a boy, it must stop here; the story could not go much further without becoming the history of a man.*

I close the book, put it into my carpetbag, and head out the door of the West Hotel. The sun is beginning to warm the air and light the cloudless sky as I make my way down Hennepin Avenue to the train station. It's such a fine fall day, and I'm on my way back to my family. I whistle as I walk.

Chapter 17

GYPSY AND PRINCE MUST KNOW we are going home because their ears perk right up and they nicker and whinny when they see me walking up to the boxcar. I'd really like to travel with them, but Mr. Larsen, the ticket agent, tells me that none other than Mr. Olsen, the vice-president of the Great Western Railroad Company, himself has arranged for a special place for me in the first class section of the train. I figure it would be awful impolite to leave that seat empty.

I decide to spend a few moments with Gypsy and Prince. I scratch Gypsy's back in just the spot she likes it best and I whisper sweet nothings in Prince's ear, telling him about all the things we will do together once we are home on our new farmstead in Saskatchewan.

When the conductor comes to fetch me, I remember how I almost hit the conductor back in Newton with a shovelful of horse manure just before the train left the station. This Minneapolis conductor, standing so straight and business-like in his fine blue suit with gold buttons, doesn't look like he might be all that familiar with horse manure, but he does have the same kind of thick moustache as the conductor in Newton did. He fingers it nervously as he waits for me and then slips a watch hanging from a silver chain out of a pocket on his vest and snaps it open.

"Train leaves in ten minutes. Best let me direct you to your seat now, Master Schmidt."

I jump down out of the boxcar and follow him along the boarding platform a spell. He stops and we climb up the four stairs into a passenger car. The conductor opens the door and I give a sharp whistle.

What a fine-looking carriage! The walls are covered in a reddish-brown wood polished so shiny I can see my reflection. I look up at the gleaming tin ceiling. It has a fancy design of flowers and vines punched into it.

The conductor shows me to my spot. It is near the front. I slide onto the dark leather seat and run my hands down the polished wooden armrests on either side. The wood smells of lemons. The long car is almost full. There's lots of fine gentleman and ladies that bring to mind the folks I saw sashaying about in the lobby of the West Hotel yesterday.

"You can hang your coat on the hook by the window, son." The conductor takes my new carpetbag and stows it tidy as can be under my seat. I sit down and look out the window.

Last-minute passengers are hurrying to get onto the train. There are young boys selling newspapers and tobacco and sandwiches and candy to folks. Makes me wonder if I should have brought some food.

Just then, I spy a girl and an older woman making their way across the platform towards the train. The girl is wearing a flowery hat and looks familiar for some reason. Both the woman and the girl carry large valises that appear to be heavy and full. The girl is using both hands to handle hers. She sets her bag down for a minute and as she glances up and tucks a wave of her brown hair behind her ear, it strikes me for a second that she looks a good deal like Annie, the girl who shared my seat on the roller coaster in Omaha. What would she be doing here?

I rub my eyes. Could it be Annie? Annie, who smelled like lilacs and made my palms sweat when her petticoat brushed my trouser leg on that roller coaster seat? The older woman who is with her has sailed ahead and now she turns back and calls out something to her younger companion.

The girl bends down graceful as a doe to pick up her valise again and walks towards the train. Imagine if it really was Annie. It can't be. She lives in Omaha, with her father.

The conductor walks through our car just then. "All settled in there, Master Schmidt? I got my instructions to take good care of you. I been told your story by my superiors and they don't want no problems till we get you delivered safe and sound to your folks. I'll be back round noon to take you to the dining car for your lunch."

The train gives a lurch and we start pulling out of the Minneapolis station. I watch as we go by a bridge with stone arches and then flour mills and saw mills that line up close to each other as books on a shelf.

I see some fancy big mansions, then rows of shanties, a grand spired church, and finally lots of tall, funny-looking buildings. I ask the conductor what they are and he tells me they are called elevators and are used for storing grain. Just think! I never even heard of an elevator before this trip and now I've seen one kind for storing grain and I've ridden in another kind that takes you up and down in buildings!

We leave the city, and the train chugs through forests and by what seems an endless chain of lakes and rivers. I slip my carpetbag out from under my seat and take out the copy of *Tom Sawyer* Mr. Clemens gave me.

I open it to the inside cover, and glance at Mr. Clemens's inscription again. I flip to the final page and read those last lines he said were meant for me. It appears Mr. Clemens thinks I'm almost a grown man. I'll be twelve come Christmas. Is that a man? Will Mama and Papa reckon I'm more grown up when they see me tomorrow? Will Sylvester and Levi stop treating me like a little brother they need to look out for now that I've been looking out for myself for so many weeks?

I read a couple chapters of *Tom Sawyer*. Tom is wicked smart and full of beans. I cotton to him right off. I laugh out loud when he gets all those children to help him whitewash the fence. I'm so taken by Tom's adventures that before I know it, the conductor is at my side, clearing his throat politely. "Time for lunch, Master Schmidt. Can I escort you to the dining car?"

I close the book and tuck it under my arm to take along. No way I want to let that story out of my sight till I find out how it ends. The dining car is right next to the first-class car so we don't have to walk far. A waiter meets us at the door and takes me to a table set all lovely, like the table last night at the hotel, with lots of different sizes of forks and spoons on either side of a gold-rimmed plate with a soup bowl in its middle. The flowers painted on the bowl are pink roses, Mama's favourite, and I think what a shame it will be to cover them up with soup. The waiter pours some water into a tall glass for me, and I'm just about to take a sip when I hear a voice I know I've heard before.

"Let's sit by the window, Grandmama." I look up. It *is* Annie, Annie from the roller coaster in Omaha! The waiter is pulling out a chair for her at the table right across from mine.

Tom Sawyer slips out of my hands and lands a little too near my plate. The cutlery clatters. Annie looks up and her eyes meet mine.

"Peter?" My heart breaks into a trot. She remembers me.

"A-Annie?" I stutter.

The older woman the waiter has just seated across from Annie fixes my face with a piercing stare and raised eyebrows.

"You know this young man, Annie?"

"Yes, Grandmama. Peter was sitting with me on the roller coaster in Omaha the night of the accident. He was so friendly and calm during that long wait for Papa to rescue us. I'll never forget his kindness to me."

Annie's grandmother's lined face softens. She gets up and glides across the aisle between the tables to shake my hand. "Thank you, Peter, for looking out for my Annie. That was an awful night. I watched with horror as that car full of young people met their tragic end and my son-in-law carried out his brave rescue."

The waiter is seating a family at the table at the end of the car. Annie's grandmother beckons to him and he hurries up.

"Could this young man join us?" she asks.

"Of course, ma'am. I'll see to it immediately." He trades my dishes and cutlery with the ones beside Annie and pulls out the chair for me. I sit down, almost wishing he'd seated me next to Annie's grandmother. My nearness to Annie means I can smell all that lilac again and it's making a mist around every thought in my brain. My heart has broken into a full gallop. Will I even be able to speak, or for that matter, eat? I take a deep breath.

I soon realize I won't have to worry. Annie's grandmother is just as talkative as Ettie, Ellie, and Eudora Schmidt were. She chatters about the weather, the time she and Annie spent in Minneapolis visiting family friends, and the convenience of train travel. Annie and I steal glances in each other's direction as her grandmother chirps on, our eyes meeting and holding for just a second each time.

We bow our heads after the waiter fills our bowls from the soup tureen and Annie's grandmother recites a prayer. As we pick up our spoons, Annie's glance holds mine for just a little longer and her eyes lead me to look across the table at her grandmother, who I discover is asking me a question.

"Where are you from, Peter, and where are you going?"

"I'm from Newton, Kansas, ma'am, and I'm headed to Drake, Saskatchewan. Have you heard of it?"

Annie and her grandmother look at each other and laugh.

"We live there!" they blurt out at almost the same time.

"You do?" I'm so surprised and happy I think my heart might jump right out of my chest and land with a splash in my bean soup.

"I thought you lived in Omaha."

"My Papa lives in Omaha and works at the amusement park," Annie says.

Her grandmother continues, "Annie's mother, my daughter Matilda, passed away when Annie was born. My Matilda and Annie's father, Chester, used to live with us in Meade, Kansas, but moved to Omaha after their marriage for Chester's work."

"So how did you land up in Saskatchewan?" I ask.

"Annie's grandfather and I immigrated to Saskatchewan with many other people from Kansas just a year after her parents moved to Omaha. We bought a farm in Drake, the town that's to be your new home. We've done rather well, if I say so myself, and we now own a meat locker business as well as the farm. I went down to Omaha after Matilda died. Since Chester had no family in Omaha to look after Annie while he worked, the best plan was for me to take Annie home with me. She and I visit her father every fall and he comes to visit Annie in Drake every spring as well."

"Don't you miss him?" I wish I could take my question back because Annie's voice sounds so sad when she replies.

"I do miss him ever so much. Papa's thinking about moving to Drake to work with Grandfather at the meat locker, but machines like the ones at the amusement park are what he knows and loves, so it would be hard for him to leave. Maybe in a few years when I'm finished school I can move back to Omaha to live with him."

"We'll see about that," Annie's grandmother says briskly. "Let's eat our soup before it gets cold."

Annie's grandmother is every bit as curious about me as Mr. Clemens was last night. Although she doesn't have a freshly sharpened pencil in hand the way Mr. Clemens did, as I tell her and Annie about my family in Kansas and my adventure-filled trip north, she seems to be filing everything away in her head in much the same way as Mr. Clemens wrote things down in his big grey notebook.

We are eating our bread pudding when Annie asks me about *Tom Sawyer*, who has been sitting on the table between us during the meal.

I tell her the book is a gift from its author, Mr. Clemens, and then I get a perfectly marvellous idea. "Say, would you like to join me in my train car? I could read one of the chapters of the book aloud to you."

"Could I, Grandmama?"

"What car are you in, Peter?"

"First class," I reply. "I'm a guest of the railroad."

Annie's grandmother pauses for what seems like forever and a day but is really just a second or two.

"We are in first class too, right near the back of the car. I guess it would be fine for you to sit together for a time," says Annie's grandmother. "I will be able to keep an eye on you from my seat."

"I'm not a little girl anymore, Grandmama," protests Annie.

"I know that, Annie, but when a young lady who cares about her reputation is in the company of a young man it is only proper for them to be chaperoned."

Annie blushes. Her grandmother's words seem to change things between us a bit. I'm not exactly unhappy about that. I hope Annie doesn't mind either.

I pick up *Tom Sawyer*, tuck him under my arm, and move to the other side of the table to pull out Annie's grandmother's chair for her. Before I can do the same for Annie, she is up and ready to go. I step back and allow both Annie and her grandmother to walk in front of me.

"Here we are," I say when we reach my seat.

Annie sits down next to the window and I slide into the seat beside her as she gives her grandmother a little wave.

"Remember I'm watching," her grandmother whispers before sailing down the aisle to her seat.

I am so excited to be alone with Annie again. It feels mighty fine. A goodly measure of fearful things have happened to me on this journey, hurtling down a ravine, almost drowning, escaping a fire, and nearly dying on a roller coaster, but I realize now plenty of good things have happened too. Things like making friends with Joe, learning about windmills from Mr. Schmidt, caring for a pet gopher family, seeing a hot-air balloon, and meeting Mr. Clemens. But nothing has been as good as sitting here next to Annie.

I open *Tom Sawyer*. I know just what part I want to read to Annie: the chapter where Tom works his way into the affections of a girl named Becky.

As I read, Annie gets so taken in by the story, I wonder if she even notices she's placed one of her hands on my leg nearest her. Her fingers lying there so light and soft seem to press through the material of my new dungarees right to my thighbone. I wonder if I will see the outline of her fingers imprinted there later. I have to muster all my willpower to focus on the words in the book and keep my voice calm.

I'd hoped my trip would end happily with me back together with my family. I never dared to think it could end even more happily with me back together with Annie too.

Chapter 18

I EAT SUPPER WITH ANNIE and her grandmother in the dining car. Over fried trout and creamed peas, Annie tells me all about the school in my new hometown of Drake. The teacher, Miss Jantz, sounds different than my teachers back in Newton.

"Miss Jantz reads us a chapter of a book each and every day." Annie's eyes sparkle and her voice rises.

"Last year, she finished two books, one called *White Fang*, about a boy searching for gold in Alaska who befriends a wild dog. I think you would have liked it, Peter. And the other was about a girl named

Dorothy, who travels to a strange land called Oz with a lion, a tin man, and a scarecrow. I'm certain Miss Jantz would lend both books to you if you'd like to read them."

"I'd be much obliged," I say.

"Perhaps we can ask her to read *Tom Sawyer* this coming year. I know the other students would love it from the parts you've read to me. And you could tell everyone how you met Mr. Twain in person."

Annie has no end of stories about her teacher.

"Miss Jantz takes us out to pick wild flowers, and we use watercolour paints to make likenesses in our notebooks. She plays the piano, and we give music concerts on the front porch of the grand home she shares with her parents. We play baseball games in the pasture next to the school. I'm a left-handed pitcher, so I can strike out almost anyone."

As I listen to Annie go on about books and music and paints and baseball, I start hoping Mama will be able to convince Papa to let me be in school at least one more year. Papa was talking about me staying home to do Herman's share of work on the farm, but I'd surely like to go to school instead. I've been finding out on this journey just how interesting the world truly is, and I'd like to learn as much about it as I can. Going to school will be a good way, too, for me to see Annie more.

After supper, when we go back to the first-class car, a miracle has taken place. Our seats have been turned into beds lined with linen sheets and covered with deep blue comforters. The stewards are plumping feather pillows for us.

I shake Annie's grandmother's hand. "Goodnight, ma'am," I say, polite as ever I can.

"Goodnight, Peter. Sleep well. Annie and I look forward to you joining us in the dining car for breakfast tomorrow morning." Annie gives me a wide smile and a little wave as she walks away with her grandmother.

The steward has left a drawstring pouch and a towel monogrammed with the letters "CPR" on my bed. I peek inside the pouch to find a toothbrush and tooth powder, as well as a comb and a bar of soap. I make my way to the water closet to wash up. I think of all those weeks I managed without such niceties and how I used to grumble when Mama made me comb my hair or brush my teeth. Now it feels real good to head to bed all clean and sweet smelling.

What with the train's wheels clacking a lullaby, and the rocking to and fro of the car on the tracks, I'm asleep in a heartbeat.

I wake when the sun sneaks through a little crack in the curtains, which the steward hasn't pulled quite shut across the window. The train has stopped, and the conductor comes through the car and sees I'm awake.

"We're in Winnipeg, Master Schmidt," he whispers to me so as not to wake the other passengers. We'll be stopped here for an hour, so if you'd like to get out and stretch your legs, you go right ahead. The

Winnipeg train station is brand new and it's a sight to behold. They worked on it night and day for four years. Best not leave the station, though. You might lose track of the time. Breakfast will be served as soon as we leave for Regina."

I make my way past Annie and her grandmother's beds as I head out the door of the first-class car. It appears they aren't stirring yet. But, my goodness, inside the station there are plenty of folks who are awake. The place is so full I can hardly move. I stand for a minute looking around.

The Winnipeg train station is grand, no doubt about it. Marble everywhere: on the floor, on the walls, and even on the giant columns holding up the high, high ceiling. The place looks like a palace, but it sounds like a noisy barnyard. I realize after a time that although the people around me are talking, talking, talking, not a one of them is talking English. I recognize a few words of German, but all the other languages are strange to me.

"Immigration Hall is over this way." I finally hear an English voice. There are men in blue coats moving through the station trying to get the people to the front doors and off to someplace called the Immigration Hall.

"Immigration Hall is out the front doors and to the right. Make your way there as quickly as possible. We've got beds and food for you. You can stay at the Hall till we've helped you find a piece of land where you can settle."

The people all look kind of scared. No wonder. If they don't speak English, they have no idea what the men are saying. A new thought streaks like a runaway train through my head. I am immigrating to Canada, but so are all these folks. I know Canada is a big country, but will there be room for all of us if this many people are arriving every day in just one city?

The crowd starts moving forward and I get caught up with them. I'm wedged between an old woman in a black dress with a colourful shawl over her head and a boy about my size carrying a bulging burlap sack that keeps bumping against my shins.

We are getting closer to the front doors. I can see a big fountain outside with bushes and flowers all around. I know I've got to get away from the crowd before they move outdoors. I don't want to go to the Immigration Hall and risk missing my train. I try to find a path to the side through the thick tangled mass of bodies.

I say, "Pardon me," but folks either don't understand or are too set on their own worries to care, so I have to push and elbow my way through the wall of people. Some push back and others yell harsh-sounding words at me that I don't understand.

I have just reached the edge of the crowd when I'm grabbed by the back of my shirt collar and a voice bellows low and rough as rocks: "What do you think you are doing, boy?" The man lets go of my collar and I face him. He's wearing one of those blue uniforms.

"Thought you'd sneak into the gentlemen's smoking room, did you, boy? That's just for first-class passengers."

"I am a first-class passenger," I say.

"*Sure* you are, boy," he says, sizing me up. "You *do* speak English. That's something rare in the station these days."

"I am a passenger headed to Drake, Saskatchewan. My name is Peter Schmidt." I pull my train ticket out of my pocket to show him. He stares at it suspiciously, but says, "Well, if that's the case, you better head back to your train, boy."

He looks up at the huge clock on the wall near the ceiling and I do too. I've never seen a clock so big. It's made of shining steel and gleaming brass.

"Looky there, young fellow. It's nearly seven o' clock. If you really are on that train, it's leaving right soon. Head up these steps here and follow the hallway to the end. Then go back down the far stairway and you'll be at the door to the tracks."

"Thank you, sir," I yell as I race away. Without all those people jamming up my path, I fly down the long hallway and bolt down the stairs and through the doors to the tracks. I spy my train right away but the first-class car is away down near the front.

Just then, the train begins to move. Ahead, I can see the conductor leaning out the door of my car waving madly at me. I start to run. My heart is pounding. I can't miss this train! Just as the first-class car is set to pass the last section of the platform I reach it.

The conductor is bending over, leaning down, and I grab his outstretched arm. I dangle for a bit as the train passes the end of the platform, but the conductor hangs on as tight as that copperhead's fangs hung onto that little baby gopher my first day on the train. With a sudden jerk, the conductor hoists me up onto the stair beside him, yanks me inside, and quickly draws the door shut with a clang.

"You gave me a fair scare, Master Schmidt," the conductor says, his moustache aquiver. "I'd have been in big trouble if you were left behind again."

I'm panting like a hunting dog when I get inside the railcar. The beds have all been turned back into seats, and Annie and her grandmother have gone to breakfast. I stop at the water closet to wash my hands and comb my hair before heading into the dining car to join them.

WE REACH THE CITY OF Regina mid-afternoon, and the conductor says we will be in Humboldt, the nearest station to Drake, by nightfall. The day passes pleasantly enough. We read more of *Tom Sawyer*. Annie and her grandmother love to play board games and have brought one along called Toboggans and Stairs. They tell me it is the Canadian version of Snakes and Ladders, but both games are new to me. We play it at our table after lunch.

Later, when we are back in the first-class car, Annie comes up to my seat with a chessboard and pieces. Now there's a game I know. My brother Herman taught me to play. We put the board on the seat between us. Annie's awful clever at chess and she easily beats me. I have a hard time keeping my wits about me while we play.

I am thinking about seeing my family again. I've missed them so much. I've never really been away from them before, and now we've been apart for nigh unto a month. I wonder if they will all come to the station. I wonder if I will look very different to them. I wonder if Mama will cry when she sees me.

The conductor tells us we will arrive in Humboldt around six. Well before that, Annie's grandmother comes to tell her to return to their seat.

"We need to get our things tidied for our arrival," she says. "Say goodbye to Peter now."

Annie turns to me and takes my hand. It feels all warm and soft in mine. "I'm so glad we found each other again, Peter." I nod, suddenly unable to think of a word to say. "I'm looking forward to seeing you in school and church and meeting your family." I nod again. "Goodbye, Peter."

"Goodbye," I whisper as Annie slowly withdraws her hand from mine and glides down the aisle towards her grandmother.

I CAN SEE EVERYONE FROM the window the minute the train comes to a stop in Humboldt. There's Mama and Papa and Sylvester and Levi and even little Alvin on Levi's shoulders so he can see over the crowd that's come to meet the train. I put *Tom Sawyer* in my carpetbag along with my new clothes and make my way to the door.

As I step off the train I hear Mama shout, "There he is! Thanks be! There he is!"

The whole family comes running towards me. Mama hugs me hard, Papa shakes my hand, and my brothers are smiling so wide you can see every single one of their teeth.

And then the questions start to tumble.

"Where you been, Peter?"

"How did you get lost?"

"Are you hurt?"

"How many inches have you grown?"

"How did they find you?"

"What was the first-class car like?"

Papa takes the carpetbag from my hand and says, firm and strong, "Now everyone, let's give Peter a chance to catch his breath. The wagon is just over to the other side of the station, Peter. Your mama's made you a fine supper and our new sod house just got the roof on yesterday, so we'll all be able to sleep indoors tonight. Be plenty of time to hear all about our Peter's adventures when we get home." Papa puts his hand sure and steady on my shoulder to guide me to the wagon.

We boys climb into the back. Sylvester and Levi each punch one of my shoulders playfully and Alvin takes my hand. The sun is going down and turning the sky all manner of beautiful colours like God decided to make a special painting to welcome me home.

I listen to my parents talking in soft voices, Mama looking back every couple minutes just to be sure I'm really there. And I really am. Home at last, and ready for more adventures in another new place. But this time alongside the people who love me and know me best.

Author's Note

SORTING THROUGH SOME FAMILY PAPERS in 2014, I discovered a short autobiography written by my grandfather's youngest sister, Alma. It begins with a story about her family's 1907 migration from Newton, Kansas, to a new home in Drake, Saskatchewan.

According to Alma, three of her brothers, including my grandfather, made the journey in separate freight train boxcars, each filled with the family's livestock. Alma writes how worried her parents were when that freight train arrived at the station in Saskatchewan and the boxcar with my grandfather was no longer attached to the train! No one seemed to know what had happened to the train car or to Grandpa.

Alma doesn't say more about my grandfather's disappearance, but we know he was eventually reunited with his family. This novel provides an imaginary explanation for the mystery surrounding Grandpa's failure to arrive in Saskatchewan with his brothers.

The 1907 railroad route Grandpa's train probably followed wound through the cities of Omaha, Nebraska, and Minneapolis, Minnesota, as well as the Lake Traverse Reservation in South Dakota. Those seemed like good places for my grandfather to have adventures.

Reading histories of Omaha and Minneapolis provided a picture of what those cities had been like in 1907. I visited Sisseton, South Dakota, and newspapers from 1907 in the public library gave a sense of what the town was like during the year my grandfather might have stayed there briefly with his distant relatives.

Excursions to local sites, including Enemy Swim Lake, where Peter almost drowns, and the Sica Hollow State Park, where Peter and his friend Joe have a scary experience, made it so much easier to write about those places, as did going up a lookout tower on Sisseton-Wahpeton land to get a view of what Peter and Joe would have seen from the top of the hill they climbed together.

I visited the Sisseton-Wahpeton Oyate Tribal Administration Building on the Lake Traverse Reservation and later conducted a lengthy interview with Naomi Parker, an Elder who grew up there.

I was so appreciative of the fact that Dr. Sherry Johnson, the Education Director for the Sisseton-Wahpeton Oyate, arranged for Winona Starrlight Burley to read my manuscript when it was complete. Winona provided me with advice that helped make Peter's time with the Little Thunder family authentic and culturally appropriate. This novel is a work of fiction but was inspired by actual people and events. Here are just a few examples.

My grandfather's name was Peter Schmidt and his older brother Herman died just before their family immigrated to Canada. Grandpa's youngest brother, Alvin, had epilepsy, and Grandpa married a woman named Annie, whose family had also immigrated to Saskatchewan.

My grandfather's family had two horses when he was growing up, Prince and Gypsy. Prince and

Peter M. Schmidt at age 16.

Gypsy's hides were saved when they died of old age, and my mother and her siblings used those horsehair blankets to keep warm when they travelled by wagon to school or church during cold prairie winters.

Mark Twain, who Peter meets near the end of the story, made several visits to Minneapolis and always stayed at the West Hotel.

Omaha's Krug Park, where Peter rides the roller coaster, was a popular attraction in 1907 and featured hot-air balloon rides, a tunnel of love, and a roller coaster called the Big Dipper.

The Dominion Immigration Hall opened in Winnipeg in 1906, right by the Canadian Pacific Railway station, just the year before Peter almost missed his train there.

There are many other things in the book that are based in fact and I'd be happy to talk about them with curious readers.

My grandfather Peter Schmidt died as a result of injuries from a car accident when I was seven years old.

I have vivid memories of my own train trips from Winnipeg to Drake, Saskatchewan, to visit him and my grandmother Annie. I remember Grandpa teaching me how to ride a bicycle and how he would flip open his pocket watch and let me listen to it tick.

I hope he would like this story I've imagined for him. Writing and researching it was a way to make my Grandpa come

Peter Schmidt and Annie Jantz Schmidt on their honeymoon train trip.

alive again for me. I hope it will also be a way for the year 1907 to come alive for the those who read this novel, so they will have a better idea about what life was like in North America more than one hundred years ago.

Study Guide

You can access this study guide with many added illustrations, suggestions, video links, resources, and curriculum outcomes on MaryLou Driedger's website at maryloudriedger.com.

Things to Do Before Reading *Lost on the Prairie*

1. Peter, the novel's hero, is going on an exciting trip! Can you recall memories of a trip using a sketch, a story, or a conversation? Do you have photographs or souvenirs to share?

2. Look at the cover of the book and the title. Write down three things you think might happen in the book. Save these predictions for when you finish *Lost on the Prairie*.

3. Learn more about the author of the book *Lost on the Prairie* on her website. Think of a question you would like to ask her.

Chapter 1

1. Peter takes the book *Captains Courageous* on his trip. What one book would you take on a trip? Explain your choice.

2. Peter's mother makes him a delicious lunch. What would a lunch with all your favourite things include? A still life is an artwork of carefully arranged objects. Can you create a still life of Peter's lunch or your favourite lunch? Check out the famous painting *Still Life with Fruit, Nuts and Cheese,* by Floris van Dyck for inspiration.

3. Peter's brother Alvin has epilepsy seizures. A seizure is when a sudden, uncontrollable surge of electrical activity in the brain temporarily affects a person's body or feelings for a period of time. Think about how you might feel if someone in your family had epilepsy.

4. Can you recreate the "fearsome racket" at the train station with a sound choir? Have friends imitate pigs squealing, chickens clucking, cows mooing, Prince and Gypsy neighing, the train whistle blowing, the conductor shouting "All Aboard," and people saying goodbye.

5. Words to think about: *ricochet, rucksack, nicker, dung, conjure.*

Chapter 2

1. List the seven things Peter liked to do with Herman. List seven things you like to do with friends. Act some out. Can your friends guess what you are doing?

2. Peter kills a copperhead snake. Make a KWL (Know-Wonder-Learn) chart for copperhead snakes. Watch a video or read a book to check the accuracy of your prior knowledge and find answers to your wondering questions.

3. How do Prince and Gypsy express their fear of the copper-head? Do people show fear differently than horses? Can you make your whole body look fearful?

4. The nail puzzle reminds Peter of his grandfather. What object reminds you of a grandparent or other older relative, and why?

5. The conductor says Peter hasn't been twiddling his thumbs on the trip. What does it mean to twiddle your thumbs?

Chapter 3

1. In Chapter 1, Peter talks about killing gophers, and in Chapter 2, he saves the lives of a gopher family. In Chapter 3, he just can't drown the gophers. What has changed Peter's attitude?

2. Watch TV news items about accidents. Write the script for a TV news report about the roller coaster accident. Remember the five W's: What happened? Where did it happen? When did it happen? Who was involved? Why did it happen? Can you perform your report like a TV reporter would?

3. What do you learn about Annie in this chapter? Can you sketch a portrait of Annie's face?

4. Phrases to talk about: *den of sin, shakes my hand like she means it, a crick in my neck, my heart foxtrots with excitement, wash my mouth out with soap, bats swoop out of the root cellar.*

Chapter 4

1. This chapter starts with a nightmare. Scary or stressful things that happen to us when we are awake can turn into nightmares when we are asleep. Experts think nightmares help us work

through difficult things that have happened to us. What are some challenging things Peter has already faced?

2. Peter realizes people and animals are counting on him. Which people or pets count on you?

3. Act out Peter's walk up the steep slope. In between each action take ten steps and rest: Using your hands, drag yourself over to an imaginary stick and use it to stand up. Get down on your bum and use your arms to move yourself a metre. Sink down and pick gooseberries to eat. Wipe the juice off your face with your sleeve. Sit down, take off your shoe, and fill it with nuts. You've reached the top, so shout "hurray"! Open the boxcar door and crawl inside.

4. Alliteration is when words that begin with the same sound are used more than once in a sentence. One example of alliteration in this chapter is *crippled crane*. Can you find at least six other examples of alliteration in Chapter 4?

Chapter 5

1. What are some hard choices Peter makes in this chapter? How does he decide what to do? Would you have made the same decisions he did?

2. A simile compares two different things, usually using the words *like* or *as*. One simile in this chapter is *He flips me up on the shore like a netted fish*. There are ten others. Can you find them?

3. Draw a picture of Peter surrounded by the things he sees underwater. Some are mentioned in the book, but can you add others? Colour your picture with crayons, then use thin blue watercolour paint to make a wash to cover the page.

4. Find images of boxcars online and try making one from a cardboard box.

5. *Lost on the Prairie* takes place over a century ago, when everyday language included words and phrases that aren't commonly used today. Here are examples from this chapter: *vex, ponder, fretful, plumb tuckered out, notion, wagon and plough horse, walk a spell,* and *land sakes*. Use context clues to figure out what they mean. Watch for other old-fashioned words and phrases as you continue reading.

Chapter 6

1. Long ago Sisseton-Wahpeton Elders used to sit with children on the shores of Enemy Swim Lake to tell the story of how the lake got its name. Find the story in this chapter. Can you research and write a paragraph about how a place in the area where you live got its name?

2. Can you find the questions Mr. Little Thunder asks to show he is concerned about Peter?

3. Peter recalls many memories of his home and family in this chapter. Can you find four of them?

Chapter 7

1. Gypsy and Peter have a special relationship. Can you think of other books you have read, movies you have seen, or stories you have heard about the friendship between an animal and a person?

2. The hill Joe and Peter climb is called Coteau des Prairies, or the Hill on the Prairie. Today it is the site of Nicollet Tower. From the tower's top, you get an amazing view of what Peter and Joe

will have seen from the hilltop. Use the description in the text to make a landscape drawing of the scene.

3. Today, Sica Hollow is a state park with a walking trail called The Trail of the Spirits. Write down five events that happen in the legend of Sica Hollow. Mix them up chronologically and see if a friend can number the events correctly.

4. Peter and Joe see a huge flock of monarch butterflies. Learn more about the annual migration of monarch butterflies by watching a video or reading a book. Look at some photos of them and try painting one.

5. Chapter 7 ends with a cliffhanger. What is a cliffhanger and why do authors use them?

Chapter 8

1. Joe is stuck in quicksand. Quicksand is a deep mass of loose sand mixed with lots of water to form a jelly-like substance. Can you make some quicksand? Try sinking objects of various weights in it.

2. Peter hears coyotes howling as he rides to get help. Coyotes howl to defend their territory, announce their presence, and call their pack together. Can you howl like a coyote?

3. Peter thinks about how his family likes to sing together. What are some of your family's favourite songs?

4. Problem-Action-Outcome are the elements of a good story. What is the problem in this chapter? What actions try to deal with the problem? What is the final outcome?

Chapter 9

1. Mr. Little Thunder learns about Peter's relatives from a Sisseton newspaper. Why might you say Mr. Little Thunder's discovery was *coincidental*?

2. What words might Peter use to describe Mr. Little Thunder and why?

3. You could say Peter has *mixed feelings* about leaving the Little Thunders. What does that mean?

4. Mrs. Schmidt owns a millinery where hats are made and sold. Three famous paintings of millinery shops created around the time *Lost on the Prairie* takes place are *The Millinery Shop*, by Edgar Degas; *The Milliner*, by Paul Signac; and *Hutladen*, by August Macke. Find them online. Which one do you like the best and why?

Chapter 10

1. Ellie, Eudora, and Ettie have preconceived and false ideas about Indigenous people. Peter's ideas differ because he has lived with a Sisseton-Wahpeton family. Can you think of a situation where you had certain ideas about people but once you got to know them your ideas changed?

2. A good paragraph has a topic sentence, relevant supporting sentences, and a closing sentence. Do some research and write a paragraph to answer one of these questions: What is quince fruit? What happens in a blacksmith shop? Can you explain how a mill grinds grain into flour? How does a rat trap work? How do you make peach cobbler? Can you explain the plot of the story about Joseph that Mr. Schmidt reads?

3. The mill has been in Mr. Schmidt's family for three generations. Can you think of some family businesses in your community? How old are they?

Chapter 11

1. Find a partner and pretend one of you is Ettie and the other one is Peter. Retell the events of this chapter from their perspective.
2. Peter has a special bond with his horses. In this chapter, Gypsy is a hero. How does she help Peter? How does Prince help him in previous chapters?
3. A metaphor is a comparison that doesn't use the words *like* or *as* the way a simile does. One metaphor for the fire in this chapter is "a stomping elephant." What other metaphors could be used to describe the fire?

Chapter 12

1. What are three questions you had while reading this chapter? How would you answer them? Ask your friends how they would have answered them.
2. Some words and phrases to talk about: *curling tongs, cinch, buckskin clothes, ledgers, toting, jabber, teetering, gingham, barn raising.*
3. Find places in this chapter where people are worried, surprised, scared, thoughtful, helpful, organized, and sympathetic.

Chapter 13

1. During the church service, Peter thinks about how many different kinds of parents there are, including the ones he has met so

far on his adventure. Some parents have problems in their lives that make it hard for them to look after their families. Have you read books or seen movies where children's parents are going through a difficult time? Has that happened in your family?

2. Peter considers what kind of grown up he might be. Can you write about what kind of grown up you will be? What kind of job might you have? What kind of family? Where would you like to live or travel? What kind of person do you want to be?

3. Mr. Schmidt and Peter take Ben's body to the undertaker. Do some research to find out what an undertaker does. Plans are made for Ben's funeral. Have you been to a funeral? What was it like?

4. Read newspaper reports about fires. Could you write one about the fire in the barn? You will need a headline. In the first paragraph give a quick summary of what happened. Add more details in the second paragraph. In the third paragraph, talk about what might have caused the fire. End with how the situation resolved.

Chapter 14

1. Listen to some of the songs Peter sings in his boxcar on the way to Minneapolis, like "Let Me Call You Sweetheart" and "Down By the Old Mill Stream," or the song "Take A Trip on An Airship," which he hears in the hotel. Try singing along with one.

2. In this chapter, Peter recalls six big adventures he has had so far. Get together with five friends and draw one frame each for a comic strip illustrating one adventure. Put your frames together to create a story about Peter's adventures.

3. Peter learns about the Eiffel Tower. There are instructions online for creating a miniature Eiffel Tower out of Lego, straws, cardboard, paper, toothpicks, popsicle sticks, or wooden skewers. Try building one.
4. Help other people learn about airships like Peter did. Do some research and create a four-slide presentation about airships.
5. Some words and phrases to talk about: *her voice can make your worries fly away, batting about, square those horses away, a heap more grown up, all at sixes and sevens.*

Chapter 15

1. Peter is fascinated by the people dressed in fancy clothes in the West Hotel lobby. Go online to see how fashionable people dressed in the early 1900s. Would you want to dress that way? Why or why not?
2. Danny is a bellhop. Can you find out how bellhops got their name?
3. Peter has never been on an elevator. Danny explains what it is. Elevators were quite new in 1907. Some things invented around the same time as the elevator were telephones, escalators, cars, radios, and movies. If you met someone who had never seen those things, how would you explain what they are and what they do?
4. Peter meets the famous writer Mark Twain in this chapter. Do some research to learn more about Mark Twain.
5. After Samson helps Peter find the West Hotel, he strides away. When Mr. Twain gets out of the elevator, he ambles down the hallway. Can you stride across a room and then turn around and amble back?

Chapter 16

1. Peter receives a letter from the railroad vice-president. Imagine Peter writes a letter back thanking him for the hotel room and telling him about the adventures he has had. Can you write the letter for Peter? Remember, a letter has a date, a greeting, several paragraphs of content, a closing, and a signature.

2. One of the books Mr. Twain has written is called *The Prince and the Pauper*. Just from the title what do you think it might be about?

3. Mark Twain's story, *The Adventures of Tom Sawyer*, has been retold in graphic novels, picture books, cartoons, video games, manga comics, theatre productions, television series, ballets, operas, more than a dozen films, and in a song by Canadian rock band Rush. Which format do you think would be the best way to retell the story and why?

4. Mr. Twain writes an inscription in Peter's copy of *Tom Sawyer*. He says the last lines in the book aren't just about Tom, they are about Peter too. How do you think those lines might apply to Peter?

5. Words to think about: *carpetbag, flyleaf, steward, surmise, condolences, succumbed, spittoon, goodly, whittle.*

Chapter 17

1. Grain elevators were used to store grain until it could be shipped across the country by train. There aren't many grain elevators left on the prairies. You can draw a grain elevator using a few simple shapes. Check out the one on the cover of this book or find others online and try to sketch one.

2. Peter wonders if his family will treat him differently now. He thinks his adventures have changed him. Do you think they have? How?

3. Personification is when a writer gives something that isn't human the ability to do something a human could. In this chapter, the author uses personification to refer to Peter's heart. Find the passage. Write some of your own examples of personification.

4. Terms to think about: *sweet nothings, sashaying, valise, dungarees, full of beans, cotton to him, stow, chaperone.*

Chapter 18

1. Peter is worried his father may not let him return to school. In 1907 only about half the children in North America went to school, and those who did often stopped attending after Grade Six. Why do you think that happened?

2. Annie and Peter play *Toboggans and Stairs* which is another name for *Snakes and Ladders*. Can you try playing *Snakes and Ladders*?

3. The letters on Peter's toiletries kit are CPR. Can you find out what those letters stand for?

4. Peter visits the train station in Winnipeg. It was built in 1906. The building is still standing and is open to the public, but it is no longer a train station. Using photos you find online, compare and contrast how the building looked in 1906 with how it looks now.

5. Peter's family lives in a sod house. Look for photos and information to learn more about them.

Things to Do After Reading *Lost on the Prairie*

1. Peter often refers to the novel *Captains Courageous*. After reading a retelling of the Rudyard Kipling novel or watching a film

version, use a Venn diagram to compare and contrast Peter's story with that of Harvey, the hero of *Captains Courageous*.

2. Draw an outline map of North America showing the provinces and states. Locate and mark Newton, Kansas; Omaha, Nebraska; Enemy Swim Lake and Sisseton, South Dakota; Minneapolis, Minnesota; Winnipeg, Manitoba; and Humboldt and Drake, Saskatchewan. Try connecting those points by drawing railroad tracks that follow Peter's journey.

3. On the author's website, read about Jacqui Thomas, who designed the cover of *Lost on the Prairie*. Can you create your own cover for the book?

4. *Lost on the Prairie* tells the story of one family's immigration to a new country. Find out if your family has an immigration story. Peter is helped by an Indigenous family whose ancestors have been living in North America for thousands of years. Find out about Indigenous roots or connections your family might have.

5. Peter is separated from his family on his immigration journey. Read some news reports about children today who are separated from their families during immigration. How do their stories compare to Peter's?

6. Pick a favourite paragraph from the book. Practise reading it aloud using a steady pace, clear diction, an interesting voice, and an expressive face. Share your passage with your friends.

7. A hero is someone who, when faced with a difficult challenge, shows courage, strength, and intelligence. Is Peter a hero? Why or why not?

Acknowledgements

I AM SO GRATEFUL TO the members of my writers' group, The Anitas, who listened to every chapter of this book more than once and offered their wise advice and endless encouragement. Larry Verstraete, Jodi Carmichael, Deborah Froese, Pat Trottier, Mindi Marshall, Melanie Matheson, Suzanne Goulden, Gabriele Goldstone, Christina Jantz, and Candice Sareen—This book would not have been published without you. Many thanks as well to McNally Robinson Booksellers in Winnipeg, who for years has graciously offered free space for our writers' group to meet.

I want to thank my husband Dave, who planned every detail of our trip to Sisseton, South Dakota, where I spent many days doing research for this book. He also organized and accompanied me on a trip to Toronto so I could attend the annual conference of the Canadian Society of Children's Authors, Illustrators and Performers (CANSCAIP). I met many writers there who provided stimulus for my work on *Lost on the Prairie*. I am grateful, as well, to the Saskatchewan CANSCAIP chapter for the professional development opportunities they sponsored, which encouraged me to push forward with my manuscript.

I have dedicated this book to my mother Dorothy Marie Schmidt Peters, but I also want to thank my father, Dr. Paul Peters. The work ethic he modelled and instilled in his children served me well as I faced the challenges of writing a novel.

My brother Ken Peters and my sister Kaaren Neufeld were early readers of my manuscript and offered affirmation and support. Deborah Froese was my first editor, and her excellent suggestions helped improve my story in ways both big and small.

I am grateful as well for the love and support of my children, Joel Driedger and Karen Leis, Bucky Driedger and Alisa Wiebe, and my grandchildren, Henri, Leo, Clementine, and Nora Dot.

Finally, thank you to Heritage House for seeing the potential in my manuscript and making its publication possible.

In 1991, our family visited Walden Pond. We were invited to write a wish on one of the rocks in a pile near the spot where writer Henry David Thoreau's cabin once stood. Our guide said rain would wash our wish into the pond and eventually it would come true. Now, thirty years later, mine has.

Pocket BIOGRAPHIES

Mao Zedong

DELIA DAVIN

SUTTON PUBLISHING

First published in 1997 by
Sutton Publishing Limited · Phoenix Mill
Thrupp · Stroud · Gloucestershire · GL5 2BU

British Library Cataloguing in Publication Data
A catalogue record for this book is available from the British
Library

ISBN 0-7509-1531-5

TM ALAN SUTTON™ and SUTTON™ are the
trade marks of Sutton Publishing Limited

Typeset in 13/18 pt Perpetua.
Typesetting and origination by
Sutton Publishing Limited.
Printed in Great Britain by
The Guernsey Press Company Limited,
Guernsey, Channel Islands.

CONTENTS

Contents

CHRONOLOGY

26 Dec. 1893	Birth of Mao Zedong.
1911	Overthrow of the Qing dynasty. Mao enrols in Republican Army.
1912	Establishment of the Chinese Republic.
1913–18	Mao at Hunan Teachers' College. Works in Beijing University library after graduation.
1919	May Fourth demonstrations in Beijing.
1920	Appointed primary school head and marries Yang Kaihui.
1921	Participates in Founding Congress of Chinese Communist Party (CCP).
1923–7	United Front between Guomindang and CCP. Mao works in both.
1925	Death of Sun Yat-sen.
1926	Northern Expedition launched by Nationalist-Communist coalition.
1927	Chang Kai-shek massacres communists and trade unionists in Shanghai.
1927	Mao Zedong leads Autumn Harvest Uprising and retreats to Jinggangshan.
1928	Zhu De's forces join Mao's in Jinggangshan. Mao and He Zizhen start to live together.

Chronology

1930	Japan invades Manchuria.
1931–4	Chinese Soviet Republic in Jiangxi. Mao largely in eclipse.
Oct. 1934	Long March begins.
Jan. 1935	Mao strengthens hold on Party leadership at Zunyi Conference.
1935	Long March arrives in northern Shaanxi.
1937–45	Sino-Japanese War.
1938	Mao marries Jiang Qing.
1945	Seventh Party Congress provides formal recognition of Mao's pre-eminence.
1946–9	Civil War between the Guomintang and the CCP.
1949	Mao proclaims the establishment of the People's Republic of China.
1953–7	First Five Year Plan, collectivization of agriculture and nationalization of industry.
1956	February, Khrushchev denounces Stalin in secret speech at 20th Party Congress.
1956–7	Hundred Flowers Movement.
1957	Anti-Rightist Movement.
1958–60	Great Leap Forward followed by famine.
1959	Peng Dehuai criticizes Mao at Lushan Conference.
1966	Outbreak of Cultural Revolution and formation of Red Guards.
1967	Liu Shaoqi and Deng Xiaoping disgraced.

Chronology

1968	Red Guards disbanded.
1969	Ninth Congress of the CCP, Lin Biao officially designated as Mao's successor.
1971	Disgrace of Lin Biao. China recovers UN seat.
1973	Deng Xiaoping returns to Beijing.
Jan. 1976	Death of Zhou Enlai.
April 1976	Demonstrations in Tiananmen, Deng Xiaoping removed from office.
9 Sept. 1976	Mao dies.
6 Oct. 1976	Arrest of Mao's wife and the other members of the Gang of Four.

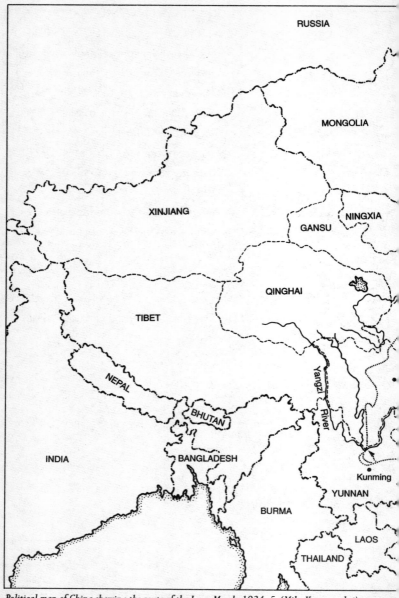

Political map of China showing the route of the Long March, 1934–5. (Mike Komarnyckyj)

Route of the Long March ⋯⋯⋯▶

INTRODUCTION

Mao Zedong was a figure of great historical importance. For most of his 83 years he was a central figure in Chinese politics. He spent the 1920s and 1930s struggling to build the Chinese Communist Party and to get his policies accepted by it. In doing so he ended its subordination to Stalin and created a Party with nationalist credentials capable of leading a successful popular revolution.

After the establishment of the People's Republic, he became a revered but rather remote leader. He strived to impose his vision of socialism on his impoverished country, convinced that if the power and enthusiasm of the people were correctly harnessed, China could become a modern wealthy and egalitarian society. His impatience with the pace of economic development under the First Five Year Plan led him to launch the Great Leap Forward. When this failed he turned on colleagues who criticized the initiative and he refused to recognize the magnitude of the disaster swamping China.

Always irascible and wilful, he now became obsessively suspicious, seeing conspiracy everywhere. He turned against many of his revolutionary colleagues and had them persecuted, imprisoned and even killed. His ideas and actions became more and more unpredictable. Yet so great was Mao's prestige that it was almost impossible for anyone to speak out against him. Even his victims participated in the most absurd manifestations of his cult, waving the *Little Red Book* and attributing almost magical powers to the study of his thought. His colleagues and members of his household became ever more preoccupied with appeasing him or manipulating his views. He in turn greatly feared the efforts of others to control him. But sycophancy did not always make people safe. Apparently loyal followers easily became suspects.

Many episodes in Mao's life are still obscure. Edgar Snow, whose book *Red Star over China* contains a biography based on interviews carried out in 1936, inevitably recorded the version of the leader's life that Mao wished to make public. Most other original sources have particular interests to advance. Mao's public utterances were often ambiguous or difficult to interpret. Debates persist among the experts over the true significance of many Party documents. All biographers of Mao have had to wrestle with these problems.

I have attempted to produce a short life of Mao that will be easily understood by readers without a prior knowledge of Chinese affairs. The task has been even more difficult than I expected. Inevitably I have had to simplify and to choose between competing interpretations of many events. Mao was a soldier, a political and military theoretician, a philosopher and a poet. He played too many parts on too large a stage for a short book to deal with the whole man. I have chosen to focus only on his political and his family life.

A Note on Romanization

I have employed the Hanyü pinyin system of romanizing Chinese words and names. Only the names of Sun Yat-sen and Chiang Kai-shek have been left in older spellings because they might otherwise be difficult for readers to recognize.

ONE

CHILDHOOD AND FORMATIVE YEARS

Mao Zedong was born in the village of Shaoshan in Xiangtan county, Hunan province, on 26 December 1893. His father, Mao Shunsheng, had become a soldier in order to clear his debts. On his return from his military service, he bought land to which he was able to add little by little over the years, by working his family hard. Industry and thrift finally allowed him to amass enough land to hire a farm labourer and become a grain trader. Mao's mother, Wen Qimei, was an illiterate peasant woman who, like other village women, had to cook, wash, sew and weave for her growing family, as well as working on the land.

Mao portrayed his father as a harsh, authoritarian figure who frequently beat his children. Mao Shunsheng had had two years' schooling and could keep accounts. His attitude to education was pragmatic. He wanted his children to learn enough to do book-keeping, and believed a mastery of the classics worthwhile because such knowledge was still useful in lawsuits. Other reading he regarded as a waste of time. Mao had to hide himself away to devour *All Men are Brothers*, *Monkey* and *The Water Margin*, great novels of adventure, rebellion and intrigue which have enraptured generations of young Chinese. He referred to these books constantly in speeches and essays throughout his life. Mao's mother was kindly and played the peacemaker in family rows. She was a pious Buddhist who sometimes incurred her husband's wrath by giving food to the poor. The children were closer to their mother than to their father. Mao had two younger brothers and a sister. We may guess that his influence on them was strong because all three later became involved in the communist movement. His sister, Mao Zehong, was executed in 1930. One brother, Mao Zetan, was killed in action in 1935 and the other, Mao Zemin, was executed in 1943.

Like other country children, Mao worked in the fields from the age of six. He was fortunate to attend primary school for about five years. At thirteen he began to work full-time on the land. Throughout his childhood Mao had conflicts with his father that he was sometimes able to win. By his own account, in arguing with his father he learned to defend his position, to negotiate, and also to obtain concessions by making threats. When he was sixteen, despite his father's opposition, Mao decided that he wanted to take up his studies again. He borrowed money for the fees and registered for a modern primary school about fifteen miles from his home. Mao was several years older than his classmates. Most of them came from well-to-do homes and he felt that they looked down on him for being poor and shabby. It must have taken courage to persevere, but he remained at this school for a year, impressing his teachers with his well-written essays. In the summer of 1911 he moved on to a school in Changsha, the provincial capital.

The humiliating defeat suffered by China at the hands of Japan in 1895 led many Chinese to search for ways to help their country regain its strength and wealth. A movement of political reform led by the gentry was suppressed by the ruling Manchu dynasty in 1898, but its advocacy of a constitutional monarchy and the modernization of government and education had a lasting influence. The Boxer Uprising of 1898–1900, a peasant movement inspired by anti-foreign feelings, ended in further disaster for China as the dynasty was forced to agree to pay huge sums in reparations for foreign lives and property. Despite half-hearted attempts to introduce reforms of its own the Manchu dynasty, under the Empress Dowager until 1908 and thereafter under a conservative regent ruling on behalf of his infant son Pu Yi, handled the pressure for change badly. By the end of the decade its prestige was at an all-time low and it fell to a republican revolution in 1911.

It is hardly surprising that Mao developed an intense interest in national heroes. He read about Napoleon, Washington, Peter the Great and Wellington, and debated the ideas of Kang Youwei and Liang Qichao, leaders of the reform movement. When he heard about the 1911 revolution, Mao dropped out of his new school, cut off the pigtail that Chinese men wore as a symbol of submission to the Manchu dynasty, and joined the local revolutionary army. He spent a few months as a private, drilling, cooking and reading newspapers. When it became apparent that the revolution had overthrown the dynasty, and that its new president, Yuan Shikai, had been successfully installed in Beijing, Mao decided to leave the army and resume his studies. For most of 1912 he read widely and drifted in and out of various schools, finding each unsatisfactory. Early in 1913 he won a scholarship to the Hunan Teachers' Training College, where he remained for five years until he graduated in 1918.

Mao does not seem to have been an easy student. He did not like the natural sciences and refused to study them. On one occasion he was nearly expelled for his part in a student protest against the mismanagement of the school. On another he grabbed by the collar a teacher with whom he was having a dispute. On the recommendation of his favourite teacher, Yang Changji, Mao read a Chinese translation of Friedrich Paulsen's *A System of Ethics*, a book which emphasizes self-control and the power of the human will. Mao clearly took the book very seriously – his marginal notes in the copy he used amount to 12,000 characters. Mao absorbed from such texts those ideas from Europe's nineteenth-century liberal tradition which seemed to him convincing or useful. The view that man is essentially good would not have been alien to anyone steeped in the Confucian classics. Mao also came to believe that human nature was malleable and could be shaped according to need, and that China could be made rich and strong by mobilizing the energy latent in each individual. Decades later the influence of such ideas was discernible in Mao's policies of mass mobilization. As a student he applied the idea of self-discipline in his daily life, dressing very simply and exercising regularly. In the summer of 1916, having decided to see whether they could live without money, he and a classmate tramped through the countryside living on whatever food the villagers gave them.

Mao's teacher Yang Changji also introduced him to the magazine *New Youth* edited by Chen Duxiu, later a founder member of the Chinese Communist Party and at this time one of China's most exciting young thinkers. *New Youth* was a major national forum for the discussion of radical ideas about how China might be transformed. In these years Mao also became involved in student organizations and in 1917, with other students, he founded the *New People's Study Group*. In 1918 some of the members of this group decided to go to France on a work and study programme. Mao, who had just graduated from the Teachers' College, accompanied them to Beijing where he obtained a job through Li Dazhao, the librarian at Peking University, to whom he was introduced by his former teacher, Yang Changji. In Beijing he fell in love with Yang Changji's daughter, Yang Kaihui. Mao's pay and living conditions were miserable, but his post brought him into contact with Chen Duxiu, the editor of *New Youth*, who was a dean at the University. It also enabled him to attend lectures by some of the most famous scholars of the day. However, Mao's efforts to strike up conversations with them failed for they were too busy to talk to a humble library clerk. There has been speculation that Mao's later harshness towards intellectuals may be attributable to the resentment he felt in this period.

Early in 1919 Mao accompanied friends to Shanghai where they were to embark for the work-study programme in France. In his own account he explained that he decided not to go with them because he wished to learn more about his own country. The fact that he was a poor linguist and lacked the money for the fare may also have played a part in his decision. From Shanghai he returned to Changsha, where he quickly became involved in politics once more. As China had declared war on Germany in 1917 and sent labourers to Europe to assist behind the front, the Chinese hoped that German concessions in China would be restored to them once Germany had been defeated; however, under the Treaty of Versailles Germany's interests in China were to be passed to Japan. The news provoked a demonstration in Beijing on 4 May 1919. The great wave of protest that subsequently engulfed the country was known as the May Fourth Movement. It included demands for the rejection of the Treaty, and also for the adoption of democracy and science in China, and the abandonment of the classical Chinese in favour of a vernacular written language that would make mass literacy possible. Mao took an active part in the movement in Changsha.

It was an eventful year for Mao in other ways. His mother died and he wrote an affectionate essay in her memory, praising her love and kindness. He took on the editorship of two student papers, both of which were later suppressed by the provincial government. In November, unhappy about the match that had been arranged for her, a Miss Chao cut her throat behind the curtains of the sedan chair which was carrying her to her bridegroom's house. Her suicide inspired Mao to published nine articles attacking the evils of arranged marriage. Although there were women members in the New People's Study Group, and many women students took part in the May Fourth Movement, educated women were still a tiny minority. In Mao's generation men were responsible for much of the writing advocating women's emancipation. The interest of young male intellectuals in what was then known as the 'Woman Question' often developed from their opposition to the arranged marriage system. Mao's personal history fits this pattern. When he was fourteen his father had arranged a marriage for him with a woman six years his senior. Mao refused to consummate the marriage or recognize it. Later, at the Teachers' College, Mao had helped a fellow student escape from an arranged marriage.

Early in 1920 Mao left for Beijing once more because his political activities had made Changsha unsafe for him. In the capital he was able to see Yang Kaihui again and to read the first part of the Communist Manifesto that had just been translated into Chinese, as well as some works about Marxism. In April he travelled on to Shanghai, where for some months he earned a living as a laundry man. In this period he was able to talk to the editor of *New Youth*, Chen Duxiu, whom Mao still regarded as a mentor. Chen's activities in the May Fourth Movement had landed him in prison. He had taken refuge in Shanghai on his release and had begun to organize a small communist group. Meanwhile, after a civil war in Hunan province, it became safe for Mao to return to Changsha. There, in 1920, with a number of friends, he established a group to study Russian affairs, a work-study group to help Chinese to go to study in Soviet Russia and a Marxist study group. He was also appointed head teacher in a primary school. That post, which he held for over two years, gave him enough financial security to marry Yang Kaihui, with whom he was to have four children.

In 1921 Mao made a third trip to Shanghai, this time to attend a meeting of delegates from the various small communist groups. This meeting is now considered as the First Congress of the Chinese Communist Party. It elected a Central Committee although Mao was not among its members. It would be some years before he achieved high office in the Party to which he would devote the rest of his life.

T W O

LABOUR ORGANIZER AND PARTY WORKER

In Hunan between 1921 and 1923 Mao engaged in a variety of political and educational activities. He set up a 'Self-study University'. Its students were provided with the occasional stimulus of a lecture from an invited speaker, and organized discussion groups, but the main emphasis was on independent reading and reflection. Despite a focus on modern learning and Marxism, traditional Chinese thought also had a place on the curriculum, reflecting Mao's belief that in adopting Marxism, the Chinese should not reject their own history and culture. Educational and political work overlapped here and some of the students later became cadres in the Chinese Communist Party.

Mao was also involved in the labour movement. This was a period of considerable labour unrest. Together with two fellow provincials, Liu Shaoqi and Li Lisan, later also to become important Party leaders, he helped to lead strikes in the mines at Anyuan in Jiangxi province and on the Guangzhou–Hankou railway. He was forced to leave Hunan again in 1923 to avoid arrest. He attended the Third Party Congress in Guangzhou in the same year and was elected to the Central Committee. This Congress was important for its discussion of the CCP's relationship with the Guomindang or Nationalist Party. Although some people, including Mao's former student and fellow labour organizer, Li Lisan, opposed it, the principle of a united front between the parties was accepted at this conference. The United Front was to last until 1927.

No single national government had achieved effective control over the whole of China since the establishment of the Republic in 1912. Instead, numerous semi-independent states, most of which were controlled by warlords, played out their rivalries in shifting alliances and civil wars. The Guomindang led by Sun Yat-sen had established its power base at Guangzhou. It was a successor organization to the groups which had overthrown the Manchu dynasty, and the revolutionary credentials of its leader, Sun Yat-sen, dated from the 1890s in Japan. Comintern policy in this period was to advocate united fronts between workers and nationalists in the underdeveloped world, and Comintern advisers in China identified the Guomindang as the progressive nationalist force with which the tiny CCP should ally. It was agreed in negotiations over the alliance that communism was not relevant to China at her level of development, that the CCP was to be allowed to keep its own identity while accepting subordination to the Guomindang, and that CCP members would be allowed to join the Guomindang as individuals. Soviet advisers assisted the Guomindang to reorganize itself along the lines of the Soviet Communist Party with decision-making powers concentrated at the top.

Mao was based in Shanghai from the time of the Third Party Congress in 1923, for he was now head of the CCP Organization Department. He was also present at the First Congress of the Guomindang and became an alternate member of its Central

Executive Committee. Under united front policies, he worked for both the Guomindang and the CCP in Shanghai, a position sneered at by communists such as Li Lisan who were opposed to the alliance. In the spring he revisited the Anyuan coalmines, still fertile ground for CCP organizers, and in the summer he spoke at the Peasant Training Institute in Guangzhou. Late in 1924 he was back in Hunan recuperating from a bout of ill health. He spent some time in his home countryside working with peasant associations until he attracted the attention of the provincial governor and was once more forced to flee. In Guangzhou in late 1925 he began to act as head of the Guomindang's Propaganda Department and directed its Peasant Training Institute. In February he became a member of the Guomindang Peasant Movement Committee.

The death of Sun Yat-sen in March 1925 left the Guomindang without clear leadership. The right wing of the party opposed the united front and began to vie for power with the left. In March 1926 Chiang Kai-shek made a bid for the party leadership by declaring martial law, arresting a number of CCP members and putting his Russian advisers under house arrest. He used his hostages to make himself leader of the Party and to obtain Russian agreement to a military expedition to the north which was intended to achieve national reunification under a Guomindang government.

As a result of this coup Mao lost his position as acting director of propaganda for the Guomindang, but he continued to work in its peasant department even when his comrades were being held hostage. He stayed in the Peasant Training Institute in Guangzhou until the end of its sixth session in October, and then returned to Hunan. At the beginning of 1927 he spent over a month in the countryside, investigating the peasant movement there. Mao's own family background had given him a familiarity with the countryside, and his work since 1925 had brought him increasingly into contact with the peasant movement. His month in the villages seems to have strengthened his belief in the revolutionary potential of the peasantry and to have made him determined to convince others of it. In a famous passage in his report on the movement he wrote:

In a very short time, in China's central, southern and northern provinces, several hundred million peasants will rise like a mighty storm, like a hurricane, a force so swift and violent that no power, however great, will be able to hold it back. They will break through the trammels that now bind them and push forward along the road to liberation. They will send all imperialists, warlords, corrupt officials, local bullies and evil gentry to their graves. All revolutionary parties and all revolutionary comrades will stand before them to be tested, to be accepted or rejected by them. To march at their head and lead them? Or follow in the rear, gesticulating at them, and criticizing them? To face them as opponents? Every Chinese is free to choose among the three, but the circumstances demand that a quick choice be made.[1]

Both the Report and an analysis of classes that Mao had published in the previous year reflect his lack of familiarity at that time with some basic Marxist positions. Revised versions in the *Selected Works* were to edit out not only his identification of the landlords as a part of the bourgeoisie, but also his advocacy of sexual freedom. Yet Mao's vision of the peasantry not only as a revolutionary class but as a class capable of leading the revolution, first spelt out in the Report, was to characterize his thought and strategy for the rest of his life. He asserted:

To give credit where credit is due, if we allot ten

points to the accomplishments of the domestic revolution, then the achievements of the urban dwellers and the military rate only three points, while the remaining seven points should go to the peasants in their rural revolution.

It was in the Hunan Report that Mao rebuked those who claimed that the peasant movement had gone too far with the memorable phrase 'a revolution is not a dinner party', later used by Red Guards seeking to justify their actions. Mao's concern for the position of women was also reflected in the Report. He commented that women, like men, suffered under three forms of authority – political, clan and religious – but had in addition to endure a fourth, the authority of men.

National events now changed the whole political balance in China. The Northern Expedition, finally launched in the summer of 1926, enabled the Guomindang and the Communists to take control of the important Yangzi city of Wuhan, where a left-leaning government was established with control over seven of China's southern provinces. Chiang Kai-shek began to plan an advance on Shanghai from his headquarters at Nanchang. The organized labour movement in Shanghai prepared to welcome the revolutionary army, causing considerable alarm to Chinese businessmen and foreigners in the city. At the end of March, as the General Labour Union called for a general strike and an armed insurrection against the warlords, Nationalist troops began to enter the city. On his arrival in Shanghai, Chiang Kai-shek attempted to calm foreign fears and held meetings with Shanghai industrialists, bankers and secret society bosses. On 12 April he began the suppression of the labour movement. Many were shot and hundreds more arrested.

The CCP was ill prepared for these events. Prompted by Stalin, whose line was a product of his struggle with Trotsky rather than of any understanding of the Chinese situation, the Russian advisers insisted that the alliance with the Guomindang had to be preserved at all costs. Many Party members were killed in the suppression of the labour movement, and the Party organization in Shanghai, its most important base, was forced underground. The CCP fell back on an alliance with the left Guomindang government at Wuhan. Even this relationship was uneasy. Many of the Guomindang leaders and the officers of their military units were from landlord families and were anxious about the radical communist land policies. The alliance collapsed in the summer, the Russian advisers fled back to the Soviet Union and Guomindang generals began a new suppression of peasant associations in Hunan and Hubei.

Under Soviet influence, Chen Duxiu was dismissed as secretary general of the CCP for 'opportunism and betrayal' and replaced by Qu Qiubai, a young member who had studied in Moscow in the early 1920s. The communists now organized a series of abortive uprisings, the Nanchang Uprising in Jiangxi in early August and the Autumn Harvest Uprising that Mao himself led in Hunan. The last of them, the Canton (Guangzhou) Commune, took place in December under direct orders from Moscow, where Stalin was anxious for a victory for his policies in China to strengthen him in his battle against Trotsky. The Commune was defeated in two days and all those identified as radicals were brutally slaughtered. By the end of 1927 the communist movement was at a very low ebb. Its organization in the cities had been crushed, many of its members were dead and the survivors had gone into hiding or fled to Moscow.

Like other leaders Mao was censured by the Central Committee for adventurism, and was deprived of his alternate membership of the Politburo and his membership of the Hunan Provincial Committee in November 1927.

Mao probably did not learn of his disgrace for some time. After the failure of the Autumn Harvest Uprising he took the survivors of his peasant army, about one thousand in all, up into Jinggangshan, the mountains which straddle the Hunan–Jiangxi border. In this isolated place he attempted to build a guerrilla base. In the course of 1928 he was joined by Zhu De and later by Peng Dehuai, both of them communist commanders fleeing with their troops after the failure of uprisings. The area was so remote that tigers and wolves still roamed the woods. Lineage organizations were strong in the five remote villages where the communist forces were based, and their policy of land redistribution encountered resistance because poor peasants identified with fellow lineage members rather than with other poor peasants. Mao was later to say of the area that it was 'exceedingly difficult for Bolshevism to take root'.[2] At the end of 1928, under the pressure of constant attack from the

Guomindang forces, Mao led his troops out of Jinggangshan across Jiangxi to the town of Ruijin on the borders of Jiangxi and Fujian. Here they set up a new communist base, the largest of about a dozen scattered through Central China, and the one which was to become the capital of the Jiangxi Soviet Republic from 1931 until 1934, when the communists were forced to evacuate it.

THREE

THE JIANGXI SOVIET REPUBLIC AND THE LONG MARCH

In Ruijin the Chinese communist leaders had a social laboratory in which they could try out their ideas. Zhu De and Mao worked out programmes of political training for the Red Army on which the politicization of Chinese communist forces was thereafter modelled. The army was put under firm political control. Soldiers undertook political study designed to instil discipline and self-respect. They were taught that as a 'people's army' they should avoid alienating the people in any way and should pay for everything they took. The Red Army, which had been recruited to a considerable extent from vagrants and bandits, became a more effective organization.

Mao made a detailed study of the rural economy of Xunwu county and attempted to relate land redistribution policies to the actual conditions he found. Some social reforms were also introduced. Marriage regulations were promulgated that forbade arranged marriage and buying and selling in marriage contracts. Divorce was to be granted at the request of either partner. Efforts were made to involve women in political matters and in support activity for the army.

There was factional struggle both within the communist area and outside it. There were purges of some of the communist bands which had been in southern Jiangxi before Mao's arrival and did not easily accept his leadership. Relations with the Party Centre were not easy either. The CCP had held its Sixth Congress in Moscow in 1928. Mao had been elected to the Central Committee but not to the Politburo. Qu Qiubai was replaced as general secretary by an obscure labour organizer, but Li Lisan soon emerged as the real leader. Li and Mao had known each other since their student days in Changsha although they had never been friends. Li had gone to study in France while Mao chose to remain in China. Later Li was opposed to the policy of the United Front when Mao supported it. Li believed that Mao failed to recognize the petty-bourgeois nature of the peasantry. On his return to China, Li began to urge Mao and Zhu De to disperse their forces and mobilize the peasant masses over the widest possible area. Mao refused and continued to build up the Red Army in the Jiangxi Soviet until by 1930 it was 60,000–70,000 strong.

By 1930 Li had changed his line, ironically enabled to do so by the new strength of the Red Army, now urging it to engage in attacks on the cities. Mao feared that his forces were not strong enough to succeed, but he finally gave way. He was political commissar and Zhu De the commander of a force which unsuccessfully attacked Nanchang in the summer. Meanwhile Peng Dehuai took Changsha and held it for a few days. Ultimately the communist armies had to retreat once more to their base areas.

Among the civilians executed in Changsha in 1930 after the communist withdrawal were Mao's sister Mao Zehong, and his wife Yang Kaihui. Yang was tortured in front of her son but would not denounce her husband. Mao's work for the revolution had made normal family life impossible and he was away for months at a time. He and Yang had spent only two years together in total. They had a daughter who took Yang's surname and three sons who took Mao's. Only the two older boys survived. Mao and Yang did not meet at all after 1927 when the communist movement in the cities was forced underground, and Mao went to Jinggangshan. From 1928 Mao lived with He Zizhen, a young middle school teacher who gave birth to six children in the nine years of their union. However, he seems always to have remembered the wife of his youth with deep affection. He recited a poem he had written in her memory to the American journalist, Agnes Smedley, in Yan'an in 1937. Almost thirty years after her death he commemorated her loyalty and heroism in another poem, 'I have lost my proud poplar'. Mao's two young sons were later reunited with him in Yan'an.

Li Lisan was now blamed for the disastrous failure of the communist assaults on the cities and recalled to Moscow where he lived in exile for fifteen years. The Party Centre came under a faction dominated by Russian-returned students who were dubbed the 'twenty-eight Bolsheviks'. In Jiangxi

Mao further consolidated his leadership in the course of the Futian Incident, a purge which involved the arrest of Li Lisan's local supporters and over 4,000 men of a Red Army corps loyal to Mao's rivals. Many details about the incident remain obscure but 2,000–3000 men are thought to have died. Mao was later to justify the action with the claim that those suppressed had been members of the Anti-Bolshevik League, but there is little doubt that he conducted it simply to defend his own power.

Moscow now adopted a new line towards the Chinese revolution, accepting the central importance of the rural soviets. The CCP's influence in the cities continued to wane and life for its urban members became ever more difficult. A series of betrayals and executions finally forced the removal of the Party centre from Shanghai to Ruijin in 1931. The rural soviets were also under pressure. Chiang Kai-shek launched five campaigns against them in the course of five years before he finally forced their withdrawal from Jiangxi in 1934. These began with the first encirclement campaign in 1930 and the second and third encirclement campaigns in 1931.

Mao's leadership came under challenge after the arrival of the newcomers from Shanghai. The

First All-China Congress of Soviets, which convened at Ruijin on 7 November 1931, the anniversary of the October Revolution, named Mao as Chairman of the Provisional Central Government of the Chinese Soviet Republic, but less than a year later, at the Ningdu conference, his strategy of drawing the Guomindang troops deep into soviet territory before accepting an engagement came under attack. Zhou Enlai, Chairman of the Party's Military Commission, and Liu Bocheng, the Chief of Staff, favoured forays outside the soviet borders and attacks on the cities to try to expand soviet territory. Zhang Wentian, one of the 'twenty-eight Bolsheviks', even demanded that Mao should be expelled from the Party but this was opposed by Zhou. Mao withdrew from the conference to western Fujian. There he fell ill and for several months received treatment from a Chinese Christian, Dr Nelson Fu, who worked at a mission hospital. Mao took an interest in the organization of the hospital and enquired about medical training. On being told that it took several years, he exclaimed that this was much too long and that a year or two should suffice. He would follow this idea through years later in his health reforms in the Cultural Revolution.

After the Ningdu conference, Mao lost much of his authority in the military sphere. In May 1933 Zhou Enlai, still a supporter of the Russian returned leadership, was appointed political commissar of the Red Army. Mao's brother, Mao Zetan, Mao's secretary and the young Deng Xiaoping were all subjected to heavy criticism in what should probably be understood as an indirect attack on Mao himself. There is some evidence that Mao was even placed under house arrest by the Party leadership in the first part of 1934.

Mao was also criticized at this time for the moderation of his land policies. Arguments about land redistribution always involve problems of what should be confiscated and from whom. Radicals argued that to satisfy the needs of poor peasants and ensure their support, not only landlords and rich peasants but even middle peasants should have their property expropriated. Mao, who had once advocated doctrinaire egalitarianism himself, now believed that prosperous peasants should be protected in order to maintain production and social stability.

However, arguments over civil and economic policy were soon to appear academic. Chiang Kai-shek's fifth encirclement campaign combined the military encirclement of the Jiangxi Soviet with an economic blockade and made the communist position untenable. In the summer it was agreed that the soviet would have to be abandoned and the evacuation was planned for the autumn. Of the 100,000 people who attempted to break through the Guomindang blockade, 85,000 were soldiers and only thirty-five were women. Most female activists were left behind with the sick, the wounded and the wives and children of the soldiers. Mao's wife, He Zizhen, although pregnant, accompanied her husband, but they left behind their children. Mao's brother, Mao Zetan, one of those left behind to defend the rear, was killed by the Nationalists after the fall of Ruijin.

The Long March on which the communist forces were now embarked had at its outset no very clear objectives. After zigzagging over about six thousand miles through some of China's most difficult terrain, it ended a year later in the communist base area of northern Shaanxi. Only one in ten of those who set out reached this destination. Many were killed in the endless skirmishes they had to fight along the way, while others fell victim to disease, hunger and exhaustion. In later years the Long March entered the mythology of the Chinese revolution. Turning defeat into victory, Party historians presented it as a great triumph from which all future generations should draw inspiration. It has been celebrated in stories, songs and films. At the time, however, it must have seemed to the participants a grim trek into the unknown.

In January 1935, at Zunyi in Guizhou province, there was a meeting later recorded as the occasion when Mao officially became leader of the CCP, but the process was probably more gradual than this would imply. Mao was named as a full member of the standing committee of the Politburo and critical resolutions passed at Zunyi reflect his views on the military strategy of the Jiangxi leadership. However, Mao was still second to Zhou Enlai in the military hierarchy.

From Zunyi the Long March moved westward into Yunnan before turning north and moving up into Sichuan and eastern Tibet. One of the best known feats of the March was the crossing of the Dadu River in Sichuan. Enemy troops had removed most of the planks from the suspension bridge. Under fire, twenty Red Army men swung across on the chains hanging high above the river, and routed the defenders on the other side. The next ordeal was the crossing of snow-covered mountain ranges reaching heights of 16,000 ft. Many of the men suffered from hunger, exhaustion and frostbite. Mao himself was ill with malaria and had to be carried on a stretcher. In northern Sichuan the Long Marchers met up with a communist group from a soviet in eastern Sichuan led by Zhang Guotao, another founder member of the CCP. The two leaders could not agree on a strategy. Zhang wanted to build a soviet on the Sichuan border because he believed that its isolation would make it defensible. Mao thought they should push further north and form a government that could organize resistance against the Japanese invaders. Eventually the communist forces split again. Zhu De remained with Zhang Guotao and his troops in west China while Mao's grouping made a last push across the dangerous swamps of the Qinghai–Gansu border, again suffering thousands of casualties. Mao finally reached northern Shaanxi in October 1936. Zhang Guotao's army suffered serious defeats in Sichuan and the survivors also later made their way into Shaanxi.

FOUR

THE NORTH-
WEST

The Shaanxi-Gansu Soviet (later the Shaanxi-Gansu-Ningxia Border Region) now became the centre of communist activity in China. It was in an area even more poor and backward than the communist border regions in the south. The staple food was millet, which many of the newly arrived southerners found hard to tolerate. The loess soil of the region, yellow and crumbly, gives the place its characteristic colour. Outsiders are always struck by the strangeness of the landscape, dominated as it is by stark eroded hills, painstakingly terraced and separated by steep gullies. Most dwellings are caves cut into the hillsides, leaving the ground above free for cultivation.

The communist capital was first Baoan and from 1937 Yan'an, a remote county town deep in the hills. The name Yan'an came to stand for the communist movement for the next ten years. Mao's home was now a two-roomed cave dwelling that he shared at first with his wife He Zichen. They had left their eldest child in the care of peasants before the start of the Long March. Their second child died in infancy and the third stayed with He's family in Jiangxi. We have a heart-rending account of her separation from him. A biographer notes that things were 'a little more difficult'[1] for her on the Long March because she gave birth and was also wounded in a dive-bombing raid. The baby was placed with a peasant family immediately and Mao never even saw her. Of all He Zichen's children only Li Min, a girl born in Yan'an, is known to have survived into adulthood.

Mao's way of life was now changing. Although still very involved with government and military affairs, he entrusted the business of fighting to others and did not leave Yan'an until 1947. He had more time to read, think and write. Translations of Marxist works were available in Yan'an and he collected around him a small group of intellectuals such as Ai Siqing and Chen Boda with whom he discussed the lectures he gave on Marxism– Leninism at the Resistance University. These were the basis of his most important theoretical works, 'On Practice' and 'On Contradiction'.[2] Re-edited versions were published in his *Selected Works* in 1952.

Edgar Snow recorded that Mao and He were considered a model revolutionary couple in Yan'an in 1936 when he was gathering material for his famous book, *Red Star over China*. However, by the summer of 1937 the marriage was in trouble. Mao had a flirtation with a young actress, Wu Guangmei ('Lily Wu'), then acting as an interpreter for the American journalist Agnes Smedley. Once again in the early stages of pregnancy, He Zizhen was furious. According to Smedley, things came to a head when He Zizhen caught Wu and Mao together late one evening and physically attacked both Wu and Smedley. Mao told his wife that her behaviour was not worthy of a communist (this has a ring of truth; her biography shows that he used the same rebuke in other quarrels) and ordered her home. He Zizhen canvassed the support of other women veterans of the Long March. Most were themselves senior Party members and many were married to top leaders. The affair was therefore potentially disruptive. It was also embarrassing because it involved a foreigner. It ended with Wu Guangmei banished from Yan'an and Smedley herself being encouraged to leave. At the end of 1937 He Zizhen also decided to go. She made her way to the Soviet Union to seek medical treatment. Her last child was born there but died in infancy. By the time He Zizhen returned to China, Mao had long since remarried.

Although Smedley confessed to being repelled by the feminine in Mao, photographs at this time show him as an attractive, commanding figure. He was tall for a Chinese, gaunt from the privations of the Long March, with a large face topped by thick black hair that he wore unusually long. A prominent black mole on his chin would have been considered a blemish in the west, but in China it was taken as a sign of good fortune. Some of his personal habits were less compelling. He did not like taking baths. (In later life he would insist on being wiped down with hot towels instead.) He smoked heavily but would never use a toothbrush, believing that drinking tea was a better way of cleaning the teeth. He spat and hawked to relieve his bronchitis. He suffered from constipation, possibly because of his addiction to sleeping pills, and frequently discussed the state of his bowels with his household.

Mao's new wife, Lan Ping, by all accounts rather fastidious in such matters, was probably more attracted by his power than his person. Twenty years his junior, she arrived in Yan'an in 1937. So well was the 'Lily Wu' affair hushed up that in some accounts Lan Ping is blamed for the break-up of his marriage to He.[3] Born in Shandong, Lan Ping's former name was Li Yunhe, but she had taken a new name, meaning 'Blue Apple', as a struggling young actress in Shanghai. In 1930s Shanghai she had had leftist connections and by her own account had joined the Communist Party. Arriving in Yan'an she used an old friendship with her fellow provincial, Kang Sheng, to obtain a job as an instructor in drama at the Lu Xun Academy. She met Mao soon afterwards and a relationship quickly developed between them. She took the name Jiang Qing, by which she was to become famous. Soon Mao decided that he wanted to divorce He and marry Jiang Qing.

Mao's new relationship brought his separation from He Zizhen to public attention and rekindled the scandal. There was sympathy for He Zizhen whose heroic sufferings during the Long March were well known in Yan'an. The women veterans of the Long March especially disapproved of the liaisons formed by male leaders with the attractive young urban women who were now arriving in Yan'an in considerable numbers. There were other problems. Jiang did not seem a suitable wife for the leader. She had had various sexual liaisons in her brief acting career and was probably not divorced from the husband she had left in Shanghai. Yan'an society was puritanical, at least where women were concerned, and the presence of exiles from the Shanghai arts world made it difficult to suppress Jiang's past. But Mao was determined to get his own way. He threatened to return to his village and live as a peasant if he could not marry Jiang Qing. In the end the Politburo agreed to the divorce and to his marriage to Jiang on condition that she had no public role. The couple married in November 1938.

Jiang Qing's only child was a daughter whom she named Li Na. Mao's two surviving children by Yang Kaihui, Mao Anying and Mao Anqing also came to Yan'an for a time. They had been sent to Shanghai after their mother's death in 1930. After the collapse of the Party organization there they lived as street children until they were rediscovered and sent to

Shaanxi. Later they went to study in the Soviet Union where they joined He Zizhen and her daughter Li Min. He Zizhen's illness was diagnosed as schizophrenia by Soviet doctors. She stayed in a Soviet clinic until her return to China in 1947. In 1949 Mao arranged for her to be cared for in Shanghai and she did not appear again in public until after Mao's death. Some rather adulatory biographical material about her appeared when Jiang Qing was being discredited. He Zizhen died in 1984.

After she returned from the Soviet Union, He Zizhen's daughter Li Min was brought up with her stepsister, Li Na. Both girls bore Jiang Qing's family name Li. In revolutionary families, children, especially girls, were often given their mother's surname as a statement of sexual equality. However, for Li Min to take the surname of the stepmother who had supplanted her own mother seems a bizarre variation of this Yan'an convention. Mao's family life during the revolution was inevitably disturbed and filled with tragedy. He had little choice but to leave his children in the care of others. After the establishment of the People's Republic, his four surviving children, his two sons by Yang Kaihui, and his two daughters, lived in his household in

Beijing where they were later joined by his nephew, Mao Yuanxin, the son of Mao Zemin.

Dramatic developments at national level in the years following the Long March changed the whole context of the communist struggle. The Japanese had occupied the three north-eastern provinces of China in 1931. Convinced that China could not stand alone against Japan, Chiang Kai-shek chose to avoid outright conflict, despite enormous provocation. The CCP's declaration of war on Japan from its remote base at Jiangxi was only significant as a gesture. But the Long March brought the communist armies much closer to the Japanese armies of occupation. The Comintern began to promote a world-wide alliance against fascism. Moreover, Chiang's unwillingness to offer any resistance to the Japanese invasion was unpopular. Chiang was kidnapped by one of his own generals in December 1936 in what became known as the Xian Incident. Its resolution, brokered by the communist leader Zhou Enlai, produced a new united front. When war with Japan finally broke out in 1937 the Guomindang and the CCP cooperated with each other. The CCP agreed to abandon its radical land reform policy in favour of one of rent reduction.

The Red Army was given a financial subsidy and the CCP was allowed to set up offices in the Nationalist areas.

This collaboration came under strain as the communists expanded their power in north China and it ended with the outbreak of hostilities between the communist New Fourth Army and Guomindang forces in 1941. It had, however, allowed the communists a breathing space. Their numbers and their territory had grown. Moreover, visitors from the outside world reached Yan'an in this period and communist forces were increasingly seen both inside and outside China as heroic resisters against fascism. Mao, who had earlier argued against Moscow's United Front policy, supported the collaboration with the Guomindang and successfully exploited the opportunities it offered. His views are set out in his 1940 essay 'On New Democracy'.[4]

In Yan'an Mao established his complete supremacy over the Chinese communist movement. The first step was to get the local leadership of the Shaanxi soviet to acknowledge his authority. When Zhang Guotao, having failed to establish a soviet in Sichuan after he parted from Mao on the Long

March, arrived in Shaanxi in 1936, he was put on trial for his errors and he defected to the Guomindang in 1938. In this period Mao was also increasingly able to assert the CCP's independence from Moscow. This had not been an issue during the Long March: radio contact with the Soviet Union, lost in 1934, was not regained until 1936. Otto Braun, a representative of the Comintern, had accompanied the Red Army but his influence was on the wane as Mao consolidated his position. Braun left China in 1937. Wang Ming, the leader of the 'twenty-eight Bolsheviks' and general secretary of the Party until he was replaced and assigned to Moscow in 1931, was sent back to Yan'an in 1937, presumably to reinforce the pro-Moscow leadership. Wang favoured a closer relationship between the Guomindang and the CCP than Mao did. Mao took his challenge seriously enough to organize a struggle against it, and Wang's position was fatally weakened by the collapse of the United Front.

Mao also used the campaign to present his 'Yan'an Talks on Art and Literature',[5] in which he set out his view that literature and art should serve politics. This, of course, implied a close control of literature and publishing. The Yan'an Talks provided the basis for communist cultural policy in which all forms of fiction, essays, novels, plays and short stories, were taken immensely seriously and authors who strayed from the 'correct line' could be severely punished.

The rectification movement of 1941–4 saw the final defeat of the returned student faction. Mao used the movement both to consolidate his position as the political leader of the Chinese communist movement and also to stake a claim to being its chief theoretician. At first this was a study campaign in which works by Mao were the core reading matter. Mao always tended to devalue book-learning and to insist on the value of education through doing. 'All genuine knowledge originates in experience,' he wrote in 1937, and 'Discover truth through practice and again through practice verify the truth'.[6] In one of these study texts he insists that shit is more useful than dogma. 'A dog's shit can fertilize the fields and man's can feed the dog. And dogmas? They can neither fertilize the field nor feed the dog. Of what use are they?'[7]

The 'dogmatists' against whom this was directed were Wang Ming and other returnees from Moscow who were accused of putting the United Front first to such an extent that they compromised the independence of the Chinese Party. The techniques used in the movement to impose political orthodoxy – small group meetings, criticism and self-criticism and written confessions – would be used in many subsequent movements launched by the CCP under Mao's leadership. Despite Mao's injunction that the principle of rectification should be 'to save the patient by curing the illness', the final phase of the movement involved confessions exacted under torture and some executions. In what was also to become a pattern, the leadership afterwards admitted that there had been excesses.

The rectification movement also involved the application of Mao's ideas to the administration of the Border Region. The end of Guomindang–Communist cooperation meant the withdrawal of Guomindang funding for communist troops and was soon followed by an economic blockade of the communist areas. At the same time a brutal Japanese counter-offensive reduced communist held territory. The CCP controlled a population of only 25 million in 1942 compared with 44 million in 1940. Mao's response was two-fold. He ordered a

drive to increase production by mobilizing the
whole population for the war effort. He also tried
to cut government expenditure by reducing the size
of the bureaucracy and the army, and ordering the
remaining cadres and soldiers to grow their own
food. Village-level enterprises using indigenous
technology produced goods that could no longer be
imported from outside the communist areas.
Peasant-led co-operatives were encouraged. Cadres
and intellectuals based in Yan'an and other
administrative centres were sent down to the
villages for political re-education. These measures
enabled the Border Regions to survive and grow. By
1945 communist-controlled areas had a population
of over 100 million. Mao never forgot the success of
this mobilization, and some of his policies after
1949 reflect a wish to repeat it.

Mao was elected chairman of the Politburo and of
the Central Committee in 1943. In 1945 he was
confirmed in his position by the Seventh Party
Congress, the first since 1928. All the members of
the new Politburo were associates of Mao, although
Wang Ming and two of his faction were included in
the Central Committee. From his position of

strength, Mao could now afford to show a limited generosity to his opponents but he made sure that the record reflected his views. The Central Committee passed a resolution on Party history, criticizing a long list of Mao's opponents for their left and right errors and asserting that the Party had gained strength and vigour under correct leadership after the Zunyi Conference. The new Party constitution contained a preamble which stated that Mao Zedong Thought (the Chinese term for Mao's theoretical contribution to Marxism-Leninism) was necessary to guide the work of the whole Party. Thus was Mao's political and ideological supremacy acknowledged.

When the Japanese surrendered in 1945, both the Soviet Government and the United States favoured a coalition government in China. Negotiations between the Guomindang and the CCP broke down in 1946 to be followed by civil war. The CCP seemed disadvantaged in terms of territory, arms and military might, but the Guomindang was tired and corrupt and had lost the will to rule. Inflation and financial scandal made it increasingly unpopular and sapped its army's will to fight. The communists by contrast had high morale and were perceived as brave and incorruptible. From 1947 onwards they began to gain territory. In January 1949 they took Beijing; in April they crossed the Yangzi and swept southwards. In October 1949 Mao Zedong stood on the rostrum of the Gate of Heavenly Peace of the old Forbidden City to proclaim the birth of the new People's Republic of China and to declare that China had stood up. He had taken decisive control over his Party, freeing it from Soviet dominance; now he appealed to all Chinese with the promise of a national revival that would free China from all foreign interference.

FIVE

THE COMMUNIST PARTY TAKES POWER

Mao became Chairman of the Chinese People's Republic, a post that he held concurrently with the chairmanship of the Party. Any biography of Mao before 1949 has to deal with Party history. After 1949 his story remains inextricably bound up with struggles within the Party, but equally becomes an important part of China's political, economic and intellectual developments. Mao's leading positions in both Party and state gave him considerable constitutional power while his prestige allowed him to ignore the collective leadership and act on his own authority when he so wished. He influenced the development of all the major policies from 1949 until his death.

Mao's essay 'On the People's Democratic Dictatorship', published in 1949, laid down some immediate policy directions.[1] The revolution would continue to rely on a bloc composed of workers, peasants, the petty bourgeoisie and the national bourgeoisie. Although the leadership of the revolution was now in the hands of the proletariat, the bourgeoisie could still participate. This formulation allowed the Communist Party to attract support from business people, professionals and intellectuals who perceived it as the only force strong enough to rebuild China.

Mao's essay also made it clear that China would 'lean to one side' or seek an alliance with the Soviet Union. This policy was adopted only after tentative soundings about obtaining aid from the West were rebuffed. The alliance caused concern to informed Chinese. They knew that the Soviet Army had pillaged north-east China four years earlier while liberating it from the Japanese and they wanted China to be able to stand up to the foreign powers. In general, the new communist government gained popular support by the tough stance it took in protecting China's national interest and ending foreign privilege.

Mao made his first visit to a foreign country in December 1949 when he travelled to Moscow to see Stalin. He spent three months there negotiating economic and technical aid for China, and arranging for the eventual transfer of some Russian assets in China to Chinese ownership. He reluctantly accepted the creation of Sino-Soviet joint stock companies for mineral exploitation in Xinjiang. The Chinese received much less than they had hoped for. Mao's Moscow experience added to his resentment at Soviet attitudes to the Chinese revolution.

The Korean War broke out in June 1950 and China entered it in October. Mao backed China's entry once the 38th Parallel had been crossed, despite opposition from colleagues anxious that their country was too weak to bear the burden this action would impose. The war put new strains on the Sino-Soviet relationship. The Chinese felt they were fighting on behalf of the whole socialist camp, yet they had to pay the Soviet Union for much-needed arms. Participation cost China dear. The People's Republic was excluded from its seat in the UN, isolated diplomatically, and left with the Soviet alliance as its sole foreign policy option. China's expenditure was US$10 billion and there were almost a million Chinese casualties.

Shaoshan, Mao's home village. (Author)

Mao with the great communist general Zhu De in Yan'an. (David King Collection)

Mao with his third wife, Jiang Qing. (David King Collection)

Mao in northern Shaanxi during the Civil War. (David King Collection)

Mao in northern Shaanxi during the Civil War. (David King Collection)

The triumphal entry
into Beijing, 1949.
(David King
Collection)

Mao, Bulganin and Stalin, 1950. (David King Collection)

Mao's *Little Red Book*. (Owen Wells)

Red Guards during the Cultural Revolution. (Reginald Hunt)

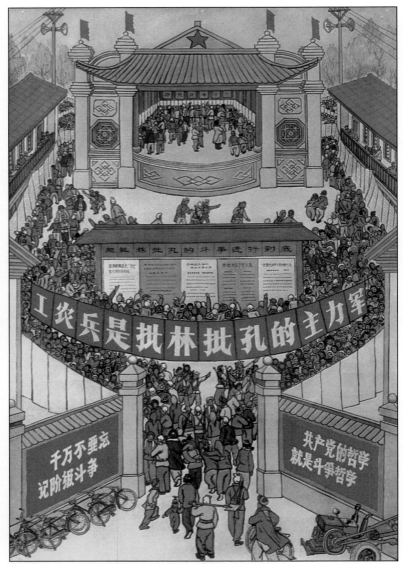

Poster, 1975. The slogans read 'Workers, peasants and soldiers are the main force in the campaign to criticize Lin Biao and Confucius', 'Never forget class struggle' and 'The philosophy of the Communist Party is a philosophy of struggle'. (Author)

Defiance of the prohibition on mourning Zhou Enlai. (Author)

Jiang Qing in the dock, 1980.
(David King Collection)

极其悲痛地哀悼伟大的领袖和导师毛泽东主席逝世

Mao's body lying in state. Jiang Qing and the other members of the Gang of Four have been airbrushed out of this print which appeared after their arrest, but their presence is acknowledged in the caption where each syllable of their names is represented by an 'x'. (David King Collection)

Mao suffered a personal loss in the war. His eldest son, Mao Anying, was killed in an American bombing raid while serving at the headquarters of Peng Dehuai, the Chinese commander-in-chief. According to one of Mao's bodyguards, Mao himself had decided that Anying should go to Korea, asking 'Who will go if my son doesn't?'. Mao's relationship with Anying had not always been easy. He had forbidden Anying to marry his sweetheart, Songlin, when she was under eighteen, the new minimum age at which women could marry, again asking 'Who will obey the regulations if my son does not?' The couple did marry when Songlin came of age and Mao's wedding gift was a heavy winter coat that he suggested that they could sleep under. Anying's death was a source of enormous grief. On hearing the news he said, 'He was Mao Zedong's son and that was his misfortune.' Soon afterwards Mao suffered another blow when his other surviving son, Anqing, was diagnosed as a schizophrenic. His illness is sometimes attributed to a beating he received from the Shanghai police when he was young. Anqing was sent to be cared for in Dalian. Apparently by a family arrangement, he married the sister of Anying's widow in 1962, and a son was born to them in 1970.

Land reform was carried out across China between 1950 and 1953, redistributing almost half of China's cultivated acreage. Mao was associated with the decision to implement a rather moderate reform that would preserve the rich peasant economy and protect production levels. In the end, however, the leadership allowed a tougher programme with an emphasis on class struggle to be implemented. It is estimated that between one and two million landlords were executed in the movement.

This pattern of initial moderation followed by radicalism was repeated in the process of collectivization of agriculture. At first it was intended to bring about collectivization by stages over a number of years, relying on voluntarism. In 1955 difficulty in procuring enough grain for the cities led to increased pressure on peasants to enter co-operatives. When it was recognized that such pressure was having negative effects on production, the policy was briefly reversed and some co-operatives were even allowed to disband. This *volte-face* angered Mao who compared its advocates to old women with bound feet holding the masses back. He convened a huge conference of peasant activists and edited their favourable reports into a volume entitled *The High Tide of Socialism in the Chinese Countryside* which was published that winter. Bypassing the formal decision-making process, he called for a speeding up of co-operativization. In the following year he pushed for even greater acceleration. By mid-1957 almost all peasants had been pressed into higher level co-operatives in which land, animals and implements were all collectively owned. Peasants were remunerated solely on the basis of the work they contributed to the co-operative. Despite the speed with which it was accomplished, co-operativization did not result in great disruption to production. Mao could therefore present it as a triumph.

In the cities in the 1950s campaigns were launched successively against counter-revolutionaries, corrupt cadres and some members of the business class accused of cheating the state. By 1956 both industry and trade were under state control. The Soviet-style First Five Year Plan, which ran from 1953 to 1957, brought steady growth rates. There were problems and bottlenecks, perhaps most notably in agriculture where investment was minimal. None the less, enough was achieved to raise public morale and to create modest improvements in the standard of living.

Intellectuals were subjected to thought reform in an effort to break their intellectual independence and discredit ideologies other than Marxism-Leninism. The process exerted intense psychological pressure and generated a tense atmosphere of suspicion and distrust. Individuals under attack were isolated, a painful state in a society that seemed overwhelmingly united in the pursuit of economic progress, socialism and national self-determination. The consequences of dissent could be tragic for both dissenters and their families.

Mao took a close interest in campaigns affecting intellectuals and played a personal role in some of them. In his essay 'On New Democracy',[2] he had condemned Guomindang censorship, its suppression of intellectuals and its oppressiveness towards all opponents. Yet in 1954 Mao joined in an attack on Liang Shuming, a writer and philosopher who advocated the blending of western-style democracy with eastern values. Liang's crime was to observe in a meeting that China's peasants led very hard lives and that the lot of the workers was easier. Mao reached for the microphone and shouted out personal invective, insisting repeatedly that Liang stank, that he was nothing but a heap of stinking bones. Liang was subsequently disgraced. Harsher still was the campaign against Hu Feng, a writer who had complained that Mao's 'Yan'an Talks'[3] were being used to justify policies that destroyed creativity in the arts. Mao himself orchestrated a campaign in which Hu was accused of leading a conspiracy to restore the Guomindang. He was imprisoned and subsequently suffered a mental breakdown. The campaign against him continued. His followers were identified, put under great pressure and punished. Their families shared their fates. This was typical of what would happen to those who were too outspoken in the future.

In an extraordinary about-turn, from the spring of 1956 Mao and some other Party leaders began to advocate a freer intellectual climate. Using the slogan 'let a hundred flowers bloom, let a hundred schools contend', they urged that academic debate should be allowed to take place without undue political interference and that the Party and officials should submit to public criticism. When the intellectuals, still cowed after the Hu Feng affair, were slow to take up this invitation, Mao urged them to overcome their fears, reassuring them that they would be treated gently. He even attacked Party leaders who were unhappy with the new policy of moderation. 'Shit or get off the pot,' he shouted at the editor of the *People's Daily* whose dilatoriness in publishing a key document Mao attributed to opposition. (The irony here, of course, is that Mao, while advocating the toleration of different views, was not prepared to tolerate any disagreement with this advocacy.)

The response began and by the early summer of 1957 some were attacking the Party and its role in fundamental ways. Under mounting pressure from colleagues, and perhaps disconcerted by the strength of the resentment he had unleashed, Mao warned against 'excesses'. Soon afterwards a new campaign of repression was launched. Almost half a million intellectuals were condemned as 'rightists' and punished with various degrees of severity. Among them were some of China's leading writers and thinkers. Educated Chinese were learning that sycophancy and conformity was rewarded, whereas the honest expression of independent thought was dangerous.

Mao's motives in launching and then reversing the Hundred Flowers Movement have been much debated. He himself later claimed that he had intended to persuade 'poisonous weeds' to reveal themselves so that they could be cut down. The truth is probably more complicated. At the beginning of 1956, foreshadowing the Great Leap of 1958, Mao was advocating mobilization for a programme of rapid industrialization. His more cautious colleagues tried to rein him back. Mao attempted through the Hundred Flowers Movement to woo the academics and managerial and technical experts whose co-operation would be required for the new economic programme. International events also influenced his behaviour. Khrushchev's denunciation of Stalin at the Twentieth Congress of the Soviet Party in February 1956 had set in motion processes of 'destalinization' in the Soviet bloc.

Mao's reaction to Khrushchev's secret speech was complex. He can have had little love for Stalin despite the eulogy he wrote on his death. Stalin's interference had brought catastrophe on the Chinese revolution in the 1920s. He had consistently backed Mao's rivals in the Party leadership, and had imposed humiliating conditions when negotiating the 1950 treaties. Mao also felt resentment about Soviet behaviour during the Korean War. On the other hand Mao was annoyed at the lack of consultation over Khrushchev's sudden disclosures and feared the turmoil that they might bring. Perhaps also he recognized that the condemnation of one personality cult could be used to challenge another. Mao's ambivalence towards Stalin and the secret speech was reflected in a *People's Daily* editorial of April 1956 which acknowledged that Stalin had made mistakes but insisted that his achievements were primary.

October brought new problems in the Soviet bloc. The Polish Communist Party was attempting to rid itself of the leaders imposed on it by Stalin. When military intervention from the Soviet Union seemed possible, the Chinese Party gave strong support to Polish Party's right to control its own affairs. Such a right was, of course, entirely contrary to Stalinist practice. The Polish episode was followed by the Hungarian Uprising in which Mao is known to have taken a close interest. In this case China supported Soviet intervention, probably because Hungary's wish to leave the Warsaw Pact was seen as a threat to the survival of the socialist camp.

Initially, the Hungarian experience did not make Mao any more inclined to embrace repression at home. On the contrary, he seems to have drawn from it the lesson that dogmatism and repressive tendencies within the Chinese party should be weeded out so that Chinese intellectuals would not turn against it. At the same time he was evidently disturbed that a communist régime had so nearly collapsed. The Petőfi Circle, the group of writers who first demanded democratic reforms in Hungary, came to stand for unreliable intellectuals in his thinking. In February 1957 he assured his colleagues that there would be no Petőfi club in China, although in 1963 he was to warn writers that they might become such a grouping. In the long run the Hungarian experience simply increased his distrust of intellectuals.

Every effort was made in the 1950s to preserve the appearance of the unity of the top Party leadership under Mao's direction. One open conflict occurred, although its details remain obscure even today. Gao Gang, leader of the Shaanxi Soviet prior to the arrival of the Long Marchers, and his subordinate, Rao Shushi, were ousted from key Party and government posts and then expelled from the Party. Their offence seems to have been an ambition to move to the highest levels of the Party leadership. Other serious disagreements took place over co-operativization and the Hundred Flowers Movement, but the mounting concern at Mao's autocratic style of leadership were successfully hidden from view.

The Eighth Party Congress held in 1956 agreed a number of measures which appeared to reduce Mao's role and stature. The reference to Mao Zedong Thought as a guide to the work of the Party was dropped from the Party constitution. The constitution attacked the myth of the infallible leader, stating that nobody is free of shortcomings or mistakes in his or her work. It also stated unequivocably that all important issues were to be decided collectively. Mao agreed to work in the second line of leadership within the Standing Committee of the Politburo, leaving the day-to-day affairs to Liu Shaoqi and Deng Xiaoping. Photographic line-ups confirmed Liu Shaoqi as second in rank to Mao and thus his heir apparent. A new post of honorary Party Chairman, created but left vacant, seemed intended for Mao when he chose to retire.

Historians differ on the interpretation of these developments. Mao's health had been poor and there was doubtless a desire to ensure a smooth transition in the event of his death or retirement. There was also a sensitivity about a cult of personality. A prohibition on naming towns, streets or factories after living leaders had been agreed by the Central Committee at the time of the establishment of the People's Republic. The Chinese leaders also signed an anti-embalming pact asking to be cremated after death. Mao is said to have agreed to the changes to the constitution and he is on record as desiring a retreat to the second line as he disliked the routine work. Some argue that these considerations are enough to explain events and insist that the Eighth Congress left Mao's dominance undiminished.

Other scholars see in the Eighth Congress a clear attempt to dilute Mao's power. The man who proposed the deletion of Mao Zedong Thought from the Party constitution was Peng Dehuai, who would confront Mao more directly in 1959. The insistence on collective leadership could be read as a criticism of Mao's style. It was presented as such in the Cultural Revolution when a Red Guard collection of Deng's 'most criminal ideas' included an extract from his report to the Eighth Congress on the new constitution:

> On all the important questions facing the Party, Leninism requires that decisions should be taken by an appropriate group and not by an individual. . . . One important contribution made by the 20th Congress of the Soviet Party was to alert us to the fact that the personality cult can lead to all kinds of disastrous consequences. Our Party has always reckoned that any party or individual can have deficiencies or make mistakes. This point is now explicitly noted in the new draft of the Party constitution. In this way our Party also repudiates the personality cult.[4]

We cannot necessarily take Mao's attitude at face value. It would accord perfectly with his character to see acceptance of a less active role and of all the other changes as a strategic retreat. As he had once written, 'when the enemy advances, we retreat'.[5] What can be asserted with confidence is that tensions already present in this period were to become far more serious from 1958 with the disastrous Great Leap Forward.

THE GREAT LEAP FORWARD AND ITS AFTERMATH

Mao visited the Soviet Union with a military mission for a second and final time in November 1957. Although he obtained a promise of help in developing an atomic bomb, it became clear that other aid would be limited. Ideological disagreements also emerged. Mao opposed the new Soviet doctrine of the peaceful transition to socialism. While Khrushchev held that in a nuclear age even local wars had to be avoided in case they turned into bigger ones, Mao argued that liberation wars were still necessary and could be limited. He further horrified the Soviet leaders by insisting that a nuclear war would not be a total disaster. Khrushchev's visits to China in 1958 did nothing to heal the breach.

The dispute convinced Mao that China would have to depend on its own efforts to become an industrial power. He became impatient with the rate of growth achieved since 1949. The developing differences with the Soviet leadership also made him more critical of the Soviet development model. Mao revived the idea of an economic leap that he had raised in 1956. His speeches in 1958 reflect his impatience with managers and planners, his distrust of intellectuals and his belief that in economic matters China could do better than simply copying the Soviet Union. Much of the language of the Great Leap Forward is quasi-military. It has been argued that the Great Leap reflected Mao's rejection of a complex new world in which leaders had to rely on experts in matters too complicated to be understood by the application of mere sense. He preferred the simpler world of guerrilla warfare where human will, enthusiasm and tenacity were the qualities that counted.

Great Leap policies affected every aspect of economic life. The overriding strategy of the movement was to substitute China's plentiful labour for scarce capital in an all-out assault on the backward economy. All peasants were reorganized into huge People's Communes, super co-operatives each with many thousands of members. Rashly, the reorganization was concentrated not in the slack season of the farming year, but in the summer. The communes practised extremely egalitarian policies that gave the peasants little economic incentive. Their massive labour forces were directed to carry out huge water control projects, many of them ill-advised. Local self-sufficiency was promoted and many new rural industries were set up. A backyard furnace movement, designed to increase steel-making capacity by starting up simple plants in every locality, was based on a naïve view of steel as the necessary basis for all industrialization. The Great Leap was also associated with an extreme anti-expert bias. To be 'red' was better than to be 'expert' and for an expert to advise that a production target was impossible was to court the label of 'counter-revolutionary'.

At first, the results of the movement seemed to be excellent. Despite the fact that many male peasants were busy making steel or working in industry, grain output was said to have doubled and similar results were claimed for industrial production. In fact, the small-scale furnaces were wasteful and inefficient. Much of the steel produced at high cost was useless. Worse still was the effect on grain production. Revised figures later showed the the 'bumper harvest' of 1958 was only 2.5 per cent higher than that of 1957. Directly affected by Great Leap policies, the harvest then fell for two years in succession. Output in 1960 was 25 per cent lower than in 1957. Yet the state continued to take grain from the peasants through tax and compulsory purchase at an increasing rate. State procurement was 17.4 per cent of the crop in 1957, 20.9 per cent in 1958, 28 per cent in 1959 and 21.5 per cent in 1960. The result was a massive famine. Death rates rose sharply. It has been estimated that between 20 and 30 million people died from the direct and indirect effects of the shortages. The Chinese press carried no reports of this tragedy. And incredibly, China remained a net exporter of grain up to and including 1960, the worst harvest year, and began substantial imports of grain only in 1961.

Who or what was responsible for this unparalleled disaster? Famine theorists have shown that famine is not brought about simply by a dearth of food; indeed, famine may take place where there is no real shortage. Access and entitlement to food are important factors and the early recognition of famine indicators is vital in mitigating the effects of shortage. Euphoria, ignorance and fear were all important factors in the Chinese famine. Reports of record outputs in one place were treated as challenges by cadres elsewhere who claimed even greater achievements. Some leaders such as Zhou Enlai, and Chen Yun, an economist associated with orthodox planning methods, had reservations about the Great Leap Forward at its inception. Others, including Liu Shaoqi and Lin Biao, appeared enthusiastic, perhaps in part at least because it was politic. At all levels from the leadership to the peasants the atmosphere of euphoric optimism made it difficult to express doubts. Mao himself, as the chief architect both of the Great Leap policy and of a political culture in which even among the top leaders no one dared tell an unpalatable truth, bears a heavy responsibility for one of the greatest disasters in human history.

In June 1959, in the midst of the disaster, Mao made a trip to Hubei. The situation there was so bad that even the state guesthouse where he and his entourage stayed had no meat on the menu. He went on to Hunan, much less badly affected, and returned to his home village of Shaoshan after an absence of thirty-two years. There he visited his parents' grave and chatted to relatives and villagers. He chided local officials who gave favourable reports of agricultural output, urging them not to exaggerate. In the evening he held a party at which the emboldened villagers began to complain about their problems: production was down and they had had to give up their pots and pans to the backyard furnaces.

In July Mao moved on to Lushan, a mountain resort in Jiangxi province, for a plenum of the Central Committee. Earlier in the year Liu Shaoqi had replaced him as head of state in a move presented to the public as just part of his retreat to the second line. Already, one witness records, many leaders, especially those who had travelled to the worst affected areas, were critical of the Leap in conversation with each other but they would say nothing that might get back to Mao. One man, however, had decided to speak up. Peng Dehuai had been with Mao on Jinggangshan and had made the Long March to Shaanxi. He had commanded the Chinese volunteers in Korea and had sent the telegram to Mao announcing Anying's death. Despite the long friendship between the two men, Peng had probably been increasingly restive about Mao's leadership style for some time. A strong, peasant-like figure, he was known to have preserved a simple life-style and was popular with the army. His manner was blunt and unsophisticated and he had a fierce temper.

Peng annoyed Mao in the first days of the conference with a challenge about the position in Hunan. A Hunanese himself, he had been appalled at the privation he had seen in his own village and Mao's on a visit earlier in the year. Subsequently, he had spoken critically of the communes to Khrushchev on a visit to the Soviet Union. Peng continued his debate with Mao in a personal letter about the Great Leap. At first sight it is a moderate text; he was careful to note the achievements and he discusses the failures as if they were collective ones. Mao had already said similar things at earlier meetings. However, Mao could say in self-criticism what he would not accept in open criticism. Although Peng did not openly attack Mao, in attacking the policies for which Mao had been responsible, he made his position unmistakable.

Mao was especially annoyed when Peng attributed the leftist mistakes of the past year to 'petty-bourgeois fanaticism'.

Mao made a decisive counter-attack. He distributed the letter to all the participants at the plenum, and made a speech in which, although he was self-critical, he reminded his audience that many others shared responsibility. He hinted that he was prepared to split the Party in this fight, but appealed for unity. With Mao in the chair, Peng was given no chance to reply. He was charged with treachery for his conversation with Khrushchev. Only his fellow marshal, Zhu De, tried to defend him. Peng lost his post as Minister of Defence and was replaced by Lin Biao. He left Zhongnanhai where all the Party and Government leaders lived, moving to a simple house on the outskirts of Beijing where he did his own housework and cultivated his garden. At first his treatment was mild. He remained nominally a member of the Politburo. In the mid-1960s other leaders including Zhou Enlai still visited him. He underwent a kangaroo trial at the hands of the Red Guards in 1966 and died in prison in miserable conditions in 1974. He was posthumously rehabilitated in 1978.

In 1960 an open split developed between China and the Soviet Union. The Russians cancelled aid agreements and withdrew their experts from China. The accusation of treachery against Peng for having discussed China's difficulties with Khruschev was now all the more damaging. Ironically Peng's stand against Mao may actually have made retreat from the Great Leap policies more difficult because of problems of losing face. The political campaign to criticize Peng in 1960 was accompanied by a new insistence on economic mobilization. The Great Leap revival met with the same difficulties as the original movement and was quickly abandoned. Liu Shaoqi and Deng Xiaoping directed a new programme that reduced the size of the communes and modified their egalitarian structure. In some cases individual farm households regained almost complete autonomy from the commune. More tolerant liberal policies were established towards literature, the arts and education. The economy recovered and food became more plentiful.

From 1961 to 1965 Mao's political power was in comparative eclipse, although he soon began to fight back. His children were by now all grown up. His relationship with Jiang Qing, already stormy in the

1940s if rumour is to be believed, had later grown more difficult. She was bad-tempered, exacting, neurotic and smug. She had spent a considerable time having medical treatment in the Soviet Union but even when she was in China she and Mao were often apart. She felt insecure in Mao's affections and resented his infidelities. Whatever the nature of their personal relationship, their political co-operation was to become stronger in the 1960s. This process had perhaps begun by 1960, for Jiang joined Mao at Lushan after Peng Dehuai had made his attack.

In 1961, according to his doctor, Mao made one of his odd sentimental gestures. When staying again at Lushan he sent for his former wife, He Zizhen, from Shanghai. He was distressed to see how old she looked and talked very gently with her for a time. After she left, he chain-smoked quietly for a long time and asked his doctor about her condition and its treatment.

In 1962 Mao began to fight back politically. While Liu Shaoqi said that 70 per cent of the problems in the Great Leap Forward were attributable to human error and 30 per cent to the weather, Mao insisted it was the other way round.

At a work conference at Beidaihe in 1962, he attacked the adjustments that had been made to bring about recovery and insisted that the Party should never forget class struggle. He even began to talk of the danger to China of following the Soviet Union's revisionist path. His study of the Soviet Union in the 1960s led him to conclude that there was no guarantee of continuous advance during the period of socialist construction. Capitalism could reassert itself and the only guarantee against this was continued class struggle. He believed that the Soviet Party had ceased to be revolutionary and that the same fate could befall the Chinese Party unless steps were taken to avert it. He pushed his line vigorously through the Socialist Education Movement from 1962 to 1964, which was intended to deal with corrupt cadres and oppose private economic activity in the countryside, and again clashed with Liu Shaoqi over the way the movement should be carried out.

Mao liked to spend long periods in south China. He preferred the climate there, but the habit also allowed him to retreat from the decision-making process when he wished and then to reproach other leaders with ignoring him. He was a poor sleeper, heavily reliant on sleeping pills, and his habit of working late at night and staying in bed until noon also made him inaccessible to visitors. Although propaganda still insisted on Mao's frugality, he led an increasingly comfortable life in his Zhongnanhai home and in well-appointed guesthouses built for him in the provinces. Each of his residences had a heated pool as Mao was an enthusiastic swimmer.

Ordinary Chinese were still unaware of differences among the leadership. Although some mistakes had been admitted, the Great Leap was not publicly repudiated. Its slogans were still to be seen everywhere. In 1964 the cult of Mao was stepped up. The radio increased its output of revolutionary songs vaunting Mao's leadership and ceased to play western classical music. Mao's name began to be mentioned with greatly increased frequency in all broadcasts. People were urged to study his Thought. His *Selected Works* was reissued. Lin Biao edited a collection of extracts from Mao's writing for the use of the People's Liberation Army. Within two years a copy of *Quotations from Chairman Mao*, more usually known in English as the *Little Red Book*, would be owned by everyone in China. In retrospect, it is clear that this new elevation of Mao was a deliberate strategy. When Edgar Snow asked Mao if there was a cult of personality in China, Mao admitted that probably there was some. 'It was said that Stalin had been the centre of a cult of personality and that Khrushchev had had none at all. Probably that was the reason for his fall.' [1]

By 1965 Mao's differences with other leaders went so deep that he decided to launch a new movement. This would involve an assault on the Party itself, for which he would rely mainly on the young. It would claim one victim after another from among Mao's oldest comrades, leaving him heavily reliant on sycophants and incompetents as he himself grew older and less competent.

SEVEN

THE CULTURAL REVOLUTION

Increasingly from 1962, Mao disapproved of the measures being taken by his colleagues to repair the damage of the Great Leap Forward and felt, in most instances correctly, that his efforts to reverse these policies were being blocked at the highest levels by colleagues opposed to his ideas. He was furious at the retreat from collectivization in agriculture and the reintroduction of material incentives. He felt that education and medicine were increasingly elitist in their development. Literature and the arts he saw as controlled by intellectuals who defied his authority. All these issues would be struggled over in the Cultural Revolution. The longest and fiercest of the great movements that Mao had set in motion since the founding of the People's Republic, the Cultural Revolution was his attempt to wrest control of the revolution back into his own hands. He himself saw it not just as a power struggle between individuals but as a struggle to restore revolutionary purity.

The opening move in the Great Proletarian Cultural Revolution (to give it its full grandiose Maoist title), came in November 1965 with an attack on Wu Han's libretto for a Beijing opera, 'Hai Rui dismissed from office'. Hai Rui (1515–87) was a Ming dynasty official, renowned for his integrity, who remonstrated with the Emperor about injustices to the peasants and was dismissed for his pains. Curiously enough, Wu Han's interest in Hai Rui can be traced back to Mao himself. At the end of 1958, Mao saw a performance in Changsha of a Hunanese opera based on an incident in Hai Rui's life. Impressed, he asked for more materials on Hai Rui and then proposed the official as a model for his courage in daring to criticize the Emperor. Wu Han, a member of the communist literary intelligentsia, was urged by a 'leading comrade' to write about Hai Rui. He responded with several articles, the first of which appeared immediately before the Lushan plenum. His libretto was staged in Beijing in February 1961.

The parallel between Peng Dehuai and Hai Rui is obvious. Wu Han's work can be read as a thinly veiled attack on Mao and as an appeal for Peng's rehabilitation. Mao arranged for the attack on the libretto, having been alerted to its pernicious nature, according to some versions, by his wife, Jiang Qing. These bare facts leave some problems. Can Mao, usually quickly roused to suspicion, really have failed at first to realize that people might identify him with the Emperor and Peng with Hai Rui? Who was the 'leading comrade' who approached Wu Han? Did Wu Han intend that his work should be read as an attack on Mao? Why did Mao leave it so long after the first staging of the play before counter-attacking?

Mao was troubled by the reluctance of low-level officials to report 'bad news' and he saw that over-optimistic claims about production made during the Great Leap were dangerous and harmful. His positive view of Hai Rui accords with his insistence on the value of honest criticism. Perhaps he was sincere when he first advanced Hai Rui as a model. However, he was also notoriously weak at accepting criticism, especially when it was directed at his leadership. At some point he began to see the use of the Hai Rui analogy as hostile to him personally. Perhaps then he used it as a means of making his enemies expose themselves. Some believe that Mao himself may have been responsible for instigating Wu Han to write about Hai Rui, or even that he had urged other leaders to study the official with the intention of giving Peng Dehuai the confidence to speak out.

Whatever the truth of origins of the Hai Rui affair, in 1965 it provided Mao with a means of attack on those high leaders whom he now regarded as his enemies. The first critical article, written by Yao Wenyuan, a Shanghai intellectual who was part of Jiang Qing's circle, appeared in Shanghai, because Peng Zhen, the Mayor of Beijing, blocked its publication in the capital. Peng believed that such a polemic should not appear without the formal approval of the appropriate Party organs. Moreover Wu Han was his protégé. Mao had already entrusted a five-man 'cultural revolution group', headed by Peng, with the task of criticizing Wu Han's play. The group's report, published in February, urged that the affair should be treated as academic rather than political, favoured lenient policies towards intellectuals and warned that some 'revolutionary leftists' were behaving like 'scholar tyrants'. Liu Shaoqi approved the report. Mao raised some specific objections to it, yet it was circulated as if it had also been approved by him. Perhaps this sealed Peng's fate. He came under harsh attack from Mao and was purged with a military leader, Marshal Lo Ruiqing, in May. The charge was conspiracy to launch a military coup. Much of the evidence was provided by Lin Biao, who had replaced Peng Dehuai as Minster of Defence in 1959.

Peng Zhen's purge was to be the first of many, as Mao removed those he regarded as enemies. An indication that there would be more came from the May 16 Circular issued by the Politburo warning against the 'representatives of the bourgeoisie who have sneaked into the Party, the government and the army'. A connection with revisionism was made by comparing such persons to Khruschev. Also in May, Mao went for a much-publicized swim in the Yangzi River, a public assertion that he was in good health and ready to fight.

Distrustful of the Party and of intellectuals Mao now turned to young people, above all to students, as his shock troops. Radical students and teachers were encouraged to criticize Party leaders, administrators and leading intellectuals. No doubt alarmed by the growing threat of chaos, Liu Shaoqi had tried to choke back student activities in the early summer and referred to Red Guard organizations as illegal. Mao by contrast proclaimed that 'to rebel is justified'. On 5 August he put up a big character poster on the door of the Central Committee building urging 'Bombard the Headquarters'. Later that month a Central Committee plenum attended by participants picked by Mao issued a directive encouraging the formation of 'mass organizations' or Red Guard groups. Liu Shaoqi lost his position as vice-chairman of the Party and sank to eighth in the Party hierarchy. Lin Biao took his place as Mao's heir apparent.

On 18 August a million Red Guards came to a rally in Tiananmen Square at which Mao appeared. Mass rallies continued until November, reinforcing the cult of Mao and his great personal authority. The movement became more and more destructive as the attack on the 'four olds' (old thought, old culture, old customs and old habits) was used to justify raids by Red Guards on private houses, and the detention, interrogation and ill-treatment of individuals. At the same time, the Mao cult became ever more intense. Between 1966 and 1968, 150 million copies of Mao's *Selected Works* and 740 million copies of the *Little Red Book* were produced. Even the victims of the movement dared say nothing against Mao and often joined their torturers in adulation of the Chairman. Red Guards collected Mao badges, sang songs such as 'the Great Helmsman' and studied his works. Ignorant of the details of revolutionary history they believed that 'China's saviour' stood head and shoulders above his old revolutionary comrades whom they were now attacking. They saw themselves as continuing the revolution and carrying out Mao's orders.

'Seizures of power' by Red Guard organizations occurred in the Shanghai municipal government, in offices and even in some of the central ministries early in 1967. Armed conflict broke out in Wuhan in July 1967 and Zhou Enlai had to be dispatched to arrange a settlement. Attacks on foreign embassies in Beijing followed and there were frequent violent incidents in the provinces. Government and Party officials came under attack in the capital and the provinces. Liu Shaoqi and Deng Xiaoping were placed under house arrest in the summer of 1967. Preposterous allegations about both men were made. Liu Shaoqi, now identified as China's

Khrushchev, was accused not only of having 'led an attack against the proletarian headquarters of Mao Zedong' after the Great Leap Forward, but also of having betrayed the revolution as far back as the 1920s and 1930s. Mao complained that Deng had not listened to him since 1959 and had treated him like a dead ancestor. Red Guards later put together an anthology of Deng's 'most criminal thoughts', many of which were statements condemning the practice of the personality cult. Now that the cult was in full flood, such utterances were proof enough of counter-revolutionary tendencies. Deng was fortunate enough to go into exile in Guangxi where he lived for the next six years. Liu was beaten by Red Guards while still nominally head of state. He died in prison two years later, weakened by ill-treatment and refused medical care. Among the many thousands of other deaths brought about by persecution were those of Peng Dehuai and Wu Han, the author of the Hai Rui play.

The campaign against Liu and Deng was organized by Jiang Qing and her associates, among them Kang Sheng, Chen Boda, and Zhang Chunqiao. They also instigated many of the attacks on other officials, intellectuals and figures in the world of literature and the arts, often in order to settle old scores. Jiang Qing finally revenged herself on the old revolutionaries who had insisted on her exclusion from political affairs when Mao married her. She also appears to have been anxious to get rid of anyone who had known her in Shanghai. Details of her colourful life at that time would certainly have undermined her reconstruction of herself as a revolutionary leader with a special relationship with the Red Guards. After Mao's death, Jiang Qing was often made a scapegoat for the worst outrages of the Cultural Revolution while Mao was in part exonerated. No doubt this was politically expedient, yet almost all witnesses agree that Jiang Qing showed particular malevolence towards her victims.

From September 1967 the Cultural Revolution was in a long slow decline, interrupted by occasional and sometimes very bloody upsurges, until the Ninth Party Congress in April 1969 marked the establishment of a new normality. The fluctuations in the movement can be directly traced to Mao's vacillating attitude. His decision to call a halt to Red Guard activities in August 1968 was influenced by growing anxiety about anarchic violence and the threat from an increasingly hostile Soviet Union. Red Guards were sent to live and work in the countryside. Revolutionary committees representing alliances between soldiers, cadres and members of mass organizations, but usually dominated by the army, were set up during 1967 and 1968 to take charge of affairs in every province, enterprise and government office.

At a national level three important groupings had vied for influence in the Cultural Revolution: the People's Liberation Army led by Lin Biao, the Cultural Revolution Group under Mao's former secretary Chen Boda and Mao's wife Jiang Qing, and Zhou Enlai and the central ministries. The army emerged greatly strengthened from the chaos. Lin Biao's promotion of the cult of Mao in the army created a personal loyalty to the Chairman which allowed him to risk his attack on the Party. Mao had then been forced to rely on the army to step into the power vacuum when he decided to end the chaos. The Cultural Revolution Group by contrast was made vulnerable by the disappearance of the Red Guards. Its members, catapulted to power by their association with Jiang Qing and their sycophancy towards Mao, lacked an independent power base. They now had to fight hard to retain the positions they had gained. Zhou and the Central Ministries appeared battered and weak. Apart from Lin Biao and Mao himself, Zhou was the only senior revolutionary leader to hold on to his position, but even he had come under attack and had been unable to protect some of his subordinates. The great majority of senior officials had been purged and the task of restoring efficient government was daunting. Yet Zhou's underlying position was strong, once Mao had decided on an end to anarchy. He and his officials were needed to restore the economy and the work of government.

Mao himself, now aged 76, appeared to have won a great personal victory. His name was accorded reverence everywhere in China. He had wiped out his enemies and claimed back the personal power he had lost after the Great Leap Forward. His ideas were in the ascendant again. The collective economy finally established in the rural areas was achieving modest success. Enterprises and government offices were nominally at least managed by revolutionary committees that included representatives of manual workers. Urban cadres were being sent down to the countryside in rotation for political re-education.

Schools and universities reopening after the Cultural Revolution introduced simplified and truncated syllabuses. Mao's belief that medical training need only take a couple of years, expressed in 1930 to Dr Fu in the mission hospital, was now put to the test. The few films, operas and novels which came out were exclusively concerned with revolutionary themes.

The cost was high. Mao had almost destroyed the Party to which he had devoted much of his life. He had negated his principle that the Party controls the gun. His regime had lost prestige both at home and abroad. The idealistic fever that the revolution had once attracted was largely replaced by a rather fearful compliance. Chinese cities were dull places. Jiang Qing's appalling model operas were unpopular and even Mao is said to have complained about Chinese films. Mao's surviving old comrades would never trust him again. He now relied for company on sycophants and retainers such as his bodyguards, his doctor and the pretty young women, secretaries, nurses and attendants, from whom he obtained care and sexual services in his old age.

EIGHT

OLD AGE AND DEATH

The Ninth Party Congress held in April 1969 appeared to make Lin Biao's position unassailable. He was specifically named as Mao's successor in the Party constitution but soon a rift began to open up between him and Mao. This rift, as yet imperfectly understood, ended in death and disgrace for yet another of Mao's successors.

In 1970 Lin Biao and Chen Boda, a leftist who had been a member of Jiang Qing's Cultural Revolution Group, proposed that the Party should formally endorse the theory that Mao was a living genius. They also suggested the revival of the post of Head of State, which had been unfilled since Liu Shaoqi's disgrace. Mao, apparently suspecting a manoeuvre to push him into retirement, rejected both suggestions. There were also differences in foreign policy. Mao was already considering the possibility of détente with the United States to which Lin was strongly opposed. Chen Boda was purged in 1970 and absurd denunciations began in 1971. Chen, a humble and devoted underling of Mao's for three decades, was now accused of dangerous ambition and was compared to Liu Shaoqi whose fall he had stage-managed.

In the summer of 1971 Mao toured the central and southern provinces of China mustering support against Lin Biao. Presumably he was especially anxious to secure the support of the regional army commanders in any showdown with his Minister of Defence. In September Lin Biao, his wife, his son and some of their associates, including in all five members of the Politburo, were killed. The official story released gradually, and with some embarrassment, over the coming months, was that the Lin family had been involved in a plot to assassinate Mao. When the plot failed, they took off for the Soviet Union in Lin Biao's personal Trident. It ran out of fuel and crashed in Mongolia. This unlikely story received partial confirmation from the Mongolian authorities who announced that a Chinese plane had indeed crashed in Mongolia with no survivors. Whatever the truth, Lin Biao's disgrace was absolute. His books, calligraphy and even the Party Constitution were gathered in and destroyed in order to eliminate all trace of the man who had stood respectfully half a pace behind Mao at so many rallies and in so many meetings. Prisoners in Beijing Qincheng prison, where many political detainees were held, learned of Lin's disgrace when their jailers collected in their copies of the *Little Red Book*. The original edition was to be replaced because it contained an exhortation written by Lin Biao to study Mao's work. The fall of Lin Biao inevitably cast doubt on Mao's judgement. How could the Chairman have chosen his successor and 'close comrade in arms' so badly? Those who still retained some idealism about the Cultural Revolution were especially disillusioned.

The remaining five years of Mao's life were characterized by a muted power struggle. The radical group, still supporters of Cultural Revolution policies, looked to Jiang Qing for leadership. They were weakened by the loss of Chen Boda and discredited by association when Lin Biao fell. None the less, with partial support from Mao, they succeeded in dominating cultural policy and fought a fierce rearguard action to retain a highly politicized approach in education with simplified curricula. Their control of the media ensured that the rhetoric of the Cultural Revolution remained current.

Radical rhetoric tended to mask the degree to which the more moderate approach of the pragmatists gained ground in other spheres. The Party and state structures were restored, economic recovery began, and many disgraced officials were allowed to return to their posts. China recovered her UN seat, and there were other foreign policy successes such as the Nixon visit. Defying the radical policy of self-sufficiency, Zhou Enlai began a modest programme of imports in support of development, including the purchase of huge artificial fertilizer plants from Japan. In 1973 the Tenth Congress of the Communist Party approved Lin Biao's posthumous expulsion from the Party. A new constitution was written in which Mao had no designated successor. Most astonishing of all, Deng Xiaoping, once named as China's second most senior 'capitalist roader', reappeared on the Central Committee. Deng began to assist Zhou Enlai who appeared increasingly tired and ill. Zhou's illness was diagnosed as cancer in 1972. His failing health complicated the power struggle between his group and the radicals, making calculations about the succession even more difficult.

Other developments at the Tenth Party Congress seemed to favour the left. Three Shanghai radicals, Wang Hongwen, Zhang Chunqiao and Yao Wenyuan, all later named with Jiang Qing as members of the Gang of Four, were given the responsibility for preparing the major Congress documents. The new Politburo and its standing committee were dominated by radicals. In 1973 a campaign was launched to 'criticize Confucius'. Although Zhou Enlai was never officially named as its target it was clear he was under attack. Jiang Qing and her associates threw themselves into the campaign, addressing meetings and rallies all over the country on the misdeeds of a statesman of the twelfth century BC, the Duke of Zhou, easily recognized as a codename for the ailing premier. However, in 1974 Zhou Enlai managed to enlarge the focus of the campaign to 'Criticize Lin Biao and Confucius' and it was wound down later that year.

Mao's role in this shadow-boxing is difficult to determine. An oscillating pattern can be traced in all his moves after 1949. He would tolerate pragmatic policies designed to promote economic stability and growth for a certain time, and would then veer to the left to launch a new movement emphasizing utopian political goals. If he detected opposition from his colleagues, he was ruthless in his determination to defeat them. As he grew older he became more autocratic and less willing to listen to their reservations. To some extent his behaviour between 1970 and his death fits this pattern. He allowed Zhou Enlai to push the new developmental programme, even protecting him at times from the attacks of the radicals. Zhou had been Mao's loyal and competent follower since 1935. A pragmatist and an administrator, he might argue against Mao's visionary policies, but once they were adopted he undertook whole-heartedly the task of trying to make them work. Even more importantly, he always supported Mao's leadership. However, the campaign to criticize Confucius must have had Mao's approval, although he may have kept it within certain boundaries. Doubtless he recognized his own dependency on Zhou Enlai's unmatched ability in day-to-day affairs and also in foreign relations. Perhaps he wanted to remind the premier that he in turn depended on Mao's goodwill. The freedom

Mao allowed the radicals to snipe at Zhou was the equivalent of allowing the guard-dogs to growl without actually unleashing them.

But Mao was also ambivalent towards the radicals. He probably approved of some of the criticisms they made of Zhou Enlai's economic policies, but despaired of their ability to govern. His personal relationship with Jiang Qing had been difficult even when they were close politically during the Cultural Revolution. They had eaten separately for many years. Often she was not allowed to accompany him on his long stays in south China. He had abandoned his earlier efforts to protect her from the knowledge of his affairs with young women. Yet he failed to defend members of his own family from her disfavour. His daughter Li Min and her husband are believed to have suffered political persecution instigated by Jiang in the 1960s and in 1972 his widowed daughter-in-law and her second husband were detained for several months for voicing criticisms of Jiang Qing.

In the 1970s personal clashes between Mao and Jiang had political implications. Jiang Qing's ambition to succeed her husband was clear. During the campaign to criticize Confucius, the Confucian attitude to women was countered by a constant insistence that women could make good rulers. Jiang commissioned essays on China's past female rulers, casting them in a positive light. Mao must have been aware of Jiang Qing's widespread unpopularity; long before her arrest, normally cautious people spoke about her with quite open hostility. Moreover he was astute enough to realize that she would be quite incapable of holding China together after he had gone.

In 1972 Jiang Qing gave a series of interviews to a young American scholar to whom she said, 'You can be my Edgar Snow.' She talked at great length about her life, her marriage to Mao, Chinese politics and her opinions on arts and literature. Transcripts were made by the Chinese and it was understood that the material would be published. Jiang probably intended to use the opportunity to launch herself as a world figure but the attempt backfired. Condemned out of her own mouth, she comes across not only as vain and selfish but also as politically naïve, astoundingly ignorant and full of deluded notions of her own popularity. When he learnt of the interviews, Mao was furious at Jiang's temerity in presenting herself as a leading figure and at her lack of discipline in talking so freely to a foreigner without authorization. It is no doubt significant that Zhou Enlai had introduced Jiang to her biographer. The highlights of the interviews were already food for gossip and jokes in Beijing in the mid-1970s although the book did not appear until after Jiang Qing's fall.

Mao may also have tired of the considerable prominence Jiang Qing enjoyed in 1974 in pursuing her anti-Confucius themes. In March their relationship was so bad that he told her it would be better for them not to see each other any more. 'You have not carried out my instructions for many years,' he complained. 'You have books by Marx and Lenin and you have my books; you stubbornly refuse to study them.'[1] By July he was even voicing his criticisms to the Politburo, referring to her wild ambitions to become chairman of the Party and calling her and her associates a Gang of Four.

In October 1974 Mao proposed that Deng Xiaoping should be given the title of first vice-premier in recognition of the fact that he was increasingly taking on Zhou Enlai's role in government. Alarmed by this victory for their opponents, Jiang Qing and Wang Hongwen tried to convince Mao that Zhou's illness was a sham and that he was plotting with Deng against the Chairman. Mao rejected their stories but restored some political balance by the appointment of Zhang Chunqiao as second ranking vice-premier. Deng was effectively in charge of the government for a little more than a year. Mao's behaviour was again ambivalent. The Gang of Four were permitted to publish their criticisms of Deng, but Deng was not prevented from pursuing policies that involved increased wage differentials and some weakening of collective farming.

In 1975 Jiang Qing moved out of Zhongnanhai and established a separate household in the complex of state guesthouses at Diaoyutai in the western suburb. Zhou Enlai left Zhongnanhai too but for quite different reasons. In June he set up his office in the Capital Hospital where he spent the last months of his life. Now it appeared that Zhou, although five years younger than the Chairman, would be the first to die. A new succession crisis loomed: who would take Zhou's place? Zhou had obviously groomed Deng Xiaoping. The radicals feared that this appointment would affect their prospects when the Chairman himself died. They launched yet another bizarre campaign, this time attacking Song Jiang, the hero of one of China's great historical novels, as a double-dealing renegade. Song was meant to represent Deng Xiaoping.

Zhou Enlai died on 8 January 1976. There was a spontaneous outburst of grief. People wore white flowers and black armbands. Many went to Tiananmen with wreaths. A film of Zhou's body lying in state was watched with intense interest and Jiang Qing's failure to remove her cap in the presence of the body caused murmurs of disapproval. There was disappointment when Mao issued no statement. An order to cease wearing mourning and to stay away from Tiananmen, presumably issued by the radicals, met with widespread defiance and the square piled up with wreaths. No announcement was made of the time at which Zhou's body would be transported to the crematorium at Babaoshan but word leaked out and a million people lined the streets in the bitter cold of the late evening to watch the cortège pass. Zhou Enlai stood for reason and restraint. It was widely recognized that he had worked hard to protect people from the worst excesses of the Cultural

Revolution and he was held in considerable affection. Now people were fearful of what would happen next.

Relief when Deng Xiaoping was picked to read the eulogy at the memorial meeting for Zhou was followed by renewed unease when Mao selected Hua Guofeng, a fellow Hunanese who had moved into the national leadership only a few years earlier, as acting premier. Hua was a compromise candidate. Mao must have calculated that he was too obscure to be strongly identified with either faction, but having been promoted during the Cultural Revolution was unlikely to turn against it. Nor was he likely to ally with Deng Xiaoping whose place he had taken.

The Gang of Four, however, saw Hua's appointment as a defeat. They began a media campaign against him and renewed their attacks on Zhou Enlai. There was a new crisis in April at the time of the Qing Ming festival when the Chinese remember their dead. Mourners again flocked to Tiananmen to remember Zhou Enlai. They posted poems in his memory, some attacking the Gang of Four. The demonstrations, seen as a demand for the return of Deng Xiaoping, were suppressed by police armed with sticks. Immediately afterwards, Mao confirmed Hua Guofeng as premier and had him made first deputy chairman of the Party. Deng Xiaoping was blamed for the disturbances and relieved of all his posts. He retreated into exile once more. In effect Mao had ceased to preserve the balance. At the end of April, Hua made a report to Mao and the Chairman signified his approval by writing the words, 'With you in charge I am at ease.' Hua was later to base his claim to be Mao's chosen successor on a slip of paper written by an old man who could no longer speak.

Mao is generally thought to have suffered from Parkinson's disease although an account by his physician claims that it was in fact motor neurone disease. Now, as his muscles wasted, he needed more and more help to walk, and communicated in grunts comprehensible only to his attendants. Prominent among them was Zhang Yufeng, once an attendant on his special train and later his mistress. She had read documents and papers to him prior to his cataract operation in August 1975. Now she nursed him, fed him and spoke for him. As he lost muscle control, his face became contorted and he dribbled. His physical appearance in the last newsreels embarrassed and disturbed people. Soon they ceased to be shown.

Zhou's death in January was followed by that of Marshal Zhu De in July. In August a great earthquake in the industrial city of Tangshan killed a quarter of a million people. There was much talk of omens. Finally, just after midnight on 9 September 1976, Mao himself died. The news was greeted with more apprehension than grief.

NINE

MAO'S LEGACIES

The first legacy of Mao to be dealt with was his body. The Politburo decided that it should be embalmed, ignoring the agreement Mao and other leaders had signed in 1956. The bloated corpse was filled with formaldehyde to preserve it in the fierce Beijing heat while a medical team desperately tried to find out about the methods used for Lenin and Ho Chi Minh. A great mausoleum was built for Mao in Tiananmen Square where for the moment he still lies.

Mao's political power passed temporarily to Hua Guofeng, whose succession was openly opposed by the Gang of Four. However, with their patron dead they did not survive long. Their failure to seek an alliance with Hua forced his hand. He could not allow the threat they posed to continue. Jiang Qing, the other members of the Gang of Four and Mao's nephew, a close associate, were arrested on 6 October. They were tried in November 1980.

Jiang Qing remained defiant to the end. She caused embarrassment by insisting that she had only been Mao's dog, barking when he told her to bark. A death sentence was commuted to life imprisonment. Ill with cancer, she committed suicide in 1991.

Hua's position was slowly undermined by supporters of Zhou Enlai and Deng Xiaoping. As pressure for the disavowal of the Cultural Revolution mounted, Hua's claim to have been chosen as Mao's successor became a liability rather than an advantage. The Third Plenum of the Eleventh Central Committee in November 1978 saw Deng's full return to power and laid the basis for Deng's reforms and a decisive rejection of Mao's vision. By the time of Deng Xiaoping's death in 1997 his policies had transformed Chinese society.

Yet Mao's posthumous fate was different from Stalin's. A total rejection of Mao would have implied a rejection of the revolution. At Deng's insistence, the official assessment of Mao expressed in a Party resolution of 1981 was balanced. Mao Zedong Thought, redefined as a product of the collective leadership, was retained as a basis for the Party's action. The resolution spoke of Mao's leftist errors as his tragedy. And having detailed the horrors of the Cultural Revolution, the resolution none the less concluded of Mao, 'if we judge his activities as a whole, his contributions to the Chinese revolution far outweigh his mistakes'. Less formally, the veteran Party economist Chen Yun mused 'Had Mao died in 1956, there would have been no doubt that he was a great leader of the Chinese people. . . . Had he died in 1966, his meritorious achievements would have been somewhat tarnished, but his overall record still very good. Since he actually died in 1976, there is nothing we can do.'[1]

The revolution that Mao led reunified China, began to modernize the economy and made the country a power to reckon with in the world. It also brought enormous improvements to the lives of many, raising life expectancy, and standards of living, and of health and education. But Mao's utopian dreams, his periodic refusal to engage with reality, his ruthlessness and his vanity also resulted in millions of deaths. His story is a vivid confirmation of the potential of power to corrupt.

The 1990s saw the emergence of a new, commercialized Mao cult. T-shirts, key rings, cigarette lighters and even karaoke videos bearing

Mao's picture have sold by the million. His image can now be used as an expression of nostalgia, a joke, a national icon, or a good luck talisman. Perhaps this reprocessing of the Chairman's image is the ultimate dismissal of what Mao stood for.

N O T E S

CHAPTER TWO: LABOUR ORGANIZER AND PARTY WORKER

1. Report of an Investigation into the Peasant Movement in Hunan in *Selected Works* (*SW*), vol. 1, pp. 23–4: Schram, *Political Thought of Mao Tse-tung*, pp. 179–82.
2. *SW*, vol. 1, pp. 99–100.

CHAPTER FOUR: THE NORTH-WEST

1. Wang Xingjuan, *He Zizhen's Road*, ch. 15.
2. *SW*, vol. 1.
3. Lan Ping arrived in Yan'an just before He's departure. However, her relationship with Mao began somewhat later. The year of Mao's divorce is disputed. According to the account given by Smedley to Edgar Snow the divorce took place at the time of the separation. I find the accounts that have Mao divorcing He in order to marry Lan Ping more convincing. The confusion may have arisen because the distinction between separation and divorce was not always clearly made in China at this time. The Chinese term for divorce, *lihun*, literally means to leave the marriage.
4. *SW*, vol. 2.
5. *SW*, vol. 3.
6. 'On Practice', *SW*, p. 308.
7. 'Reform in Learning, the Party and Literature', in Boyd Compton (ed.), *Mao's China*, p. 22.

CHAPTER FIVE: THE COMMUNIST PARTY TAKES POWER

1. *SW*, vol. 4.
2. *SW*, vol. 2.
3. *SW*, vol. 3.

4. Quoted in Simon Leys, *The Emperor's New Clothes*, pp. 167–8.
5. 'A Single Spark can start a Prairie Fire', *SW*, vol. 1, p.124.

CHAPTER SIX: THE GREAT LEAP FORWARD AND ITS AFTERMATH

1. Edgar Snow, *The Long Revolution*, p. 205.

CHAPTER EIGHT: OLD AGE AND DEATH

1. Roderick MacFarquhar, 'The succession to Mao and the end of Maoism', p. 349.

CHAPTER NINE: MAO'S LEGACIES

1. Roger Garside, *Coming Alive: China after Mao*, p. 206.

BIBLIOGRAPHY

Barmé, Geremie, *Shades of Mao: The Postumous Cult of the Great Leader*, Armonk, New York, M.E. Sharpe, 1996

Chen, Jerome, *Mao and the Chinese Revolution*, Oxford University Press, 1965

—— (ed.), *Mao Papers*, Oxford University Press, 1970

Compton, Boyd, *Mao's China: Party Reform Documents, 1942–4*, Seattle, University of Washington Press, 1952

Garside, Roger, *Coming Alive: China after Mao*, André Deutsch, 1981

Harding, Harry, 'The Chinese State in Crisis', in the *Cambridge History of China*, vol. 15, Cambridge University Press, 1991

Hollingworth, Clare, *Mao and the Men Against Him*, Jonathan Cape, 1984

Hua Chang-ming, *La Condition Féminine et les Communistes Chinois en Action, Yan'an 1935–1946*, Paris, Centre de Recherches et de Documentation sur la Chine Contemporaine, 1981

Jing Fu Zi, *Mao Zedong and his women* (in Chinese), United Publishing House, Taibei, 1991

Leys, Simon, *The Chairman's New Clothes: Mao and the Cultural Revolution*, Allison & Busby, 1977

——, *Broken Images*, Allison & Busby, 1979

Li Rui, *Comrade Mao's Early Revolutionary Activities* (in Chinese), Beijing, 1957

——, *True Record of the Lushan Conference* (in Chinese), Beijing, Chunqiu Publishing House, 1989

Li Zhisui, *The Private Life of Chairman Mao*, Chatto & Windus, 1994

MacFarquhar, Roderick, *The Origins of the Cultural Revolution*, vols 1 and 2, Oxford University Press, 1974, 1983

——, 'The Succession to Mao and the End of Maoism', in the *Cambridge History of China*, vol. 15, Cambridge University Press, 1991

Bibliography

———, Timothy Cheek & Eugene Wu, *The Secret Speeches of Chairman Mao: from the Hundred Flowers to the Great Leap Forward*, Cambridge Mass., Harvard University Press, 1989

MacKinnon, J. & S., *Agnes Smedley: the Life and Times of an American Radical*, Virago, 1988

Mao Zedong, *Selected Works*, Beijing, Foreign Languages Press, 1961

Quan Yuanchi, *Mao Zedong, Man not God*, Beijing, Foreign Languages Press, 1992

Rice, Edward, *Mao's Way*, Berkeley, University of California Press, 1974

Salisbury, Harrison, *The New Emperors, Mao and Deng*, HarperCollins, 1993

Schram, Stuart, *Mao Tse-tung*, Penguin, 1967

———, *The Political Thought of Mao Tse-tung*, Pall Mall Press, 1969

———, *Mao Tse-tung Unrehearsed, Talks and Letters: 1956–71*, Penguin, 1974

———, 'Mao Tse-tung's Thought from 1949–76' in the *Cambridge History of China*, vol. 15, Cambridge University Press, 1991

Siao-yu, *Mao Tse-tung and I were Beggars*, Syracuse University Press, 1959

Snow, Edgar, *Red Star over China*, Victor Gollancz, 1937

———, *Red China Today*, Penguin, 1970

———, *The Long Revolution*, Random House, 1972

Spence, Jonathan, *The Search for Modern China*, W.W. Norton, 1990

Teiwes, Frederick, 'Seeking the Historical Mao', *China Quarterly*, 145, March 1996

Terrill, Ross, *The White-boned Demon, A Biography of Madame Mao Zedong*, Heinemann, 1984

Wang Xingjuan, *He Zizhen's Road* (in Chinese), Beijing, Writers' Publishing House, 1981

Witke, Roxane, 'Mao Tse-tung, Women and Suicide', *China Quarterly*, No. 31, July–Sept., 1967

———, *Comrade Chiang Ching*, Boston, Little Brown, 1977

Wilson, Dick (ed.), *Mao Tse-tung in the Scales of History*, Cambridge University Press, 1977

INDEX

Index

POCKET BIOGRAPHIES

This series looks at the lives of those who have played a significant part in our history – from musicians to explorers, from scientists to entertainers, from writers to philosophers, from politicians to monarchs throughout the world. Concise and highly readable, with black and white plates, chronology and bibliography, these books will appeal to students and general readers alike.

Available

Beethoven
Anne Pimlott Baker

Scott of the Antarctic
Michael De-la-Noy

Alexander the Great
E.E. Rice

Sigmund Freud
Stephen Wilson

Marilyn Monroe
Sheridan Morley and
Ruth Leon

Rasputin
Harold Shukman

Jane Austen
Helen Lefroy

POCKET BIOGRAPHIES

Forthcoming

Marie and Pierre Curie
John Senior

Ellen Terry
Moira Shearer

David Livingstone
Christine Nicholls

Margot Fonteyn
Alistair Macauley

Winston Churchill
Robert Blake

Abraham Lincoln
H.G. Pitt

Charles Dickens
Catherine Peters

Enid Blyton
George Greenfield